I0660751

Charles Thomas Clement James

An Early Frost And An Awkward Affair

Charles Thomas Clement James

An Early Frost And An Awkward Affair

ISBN/EAN: 9783337735425

Printed in Europe, USA, Canada, Australia, Japan

Cover: Foto ©Andreas Hilbeck / pixelio.de

More available books at **www.hansebooks.com**

ROWLANDS' ODONTO
THE BEST TOOTH POWDER.

Whitens the teeth, prevents decay, gives pleasing fragrance to the breath.

ROWLANDS' MACASSAR OIL

The best preserver and beautifier of the Hair, and is the best Brillantine for the Beard, Whiskers, and Moustaches. It is now also prepared in a

GOLDEN COLOUR

for fair-haired ladies and children.

Sizes 3s. 6d., 7s., 10s. 6d. Sold Everywhere.

NOW READY

In One Vol., Crown 8vo., Cloth Gilt, 2/6

F. M. ALLEN'S NEW HUMOROUS BOOK,

"FROM THE GREEN BAG,"

By F. M. ALLEN.

By the same Author,

THROUGH GREEN GLASSES,
2/- Boards, 2/6 Cloth.

THE VOYAGE OF THE ARK,
1/- Paper, 1/6 Cloth.

ANCHOR WATCH YARNS,
Three Shillings and Sixpence.

WARD & DOWNEY, 12, York Street, Covent Garden, W.C.

WARD & DOWNEY'S CHEAP NOVELS.

SIX SHILLING NOVELS.

THE WYVERN MYSTERY. By J. SHERIDAN LE FANU:
DESPERATE REMEDIES. By THOMAS HARDY.
THE MASTER OF RYLANDS. By Mrs. G. LEWIS LEEDS.
MRS. RUMBOLD'S SECRET. By Mrs. MACQUOID.
THE NUN'S CURSE. By Mrs. R̲——

Emory University Library

In Memoriam

Ruth Candler Lovett

1935-1964

IVE.

awn."

VELS.

RJEON.
ILTON AIDE.

h of Kildare.

A RECOILING VENGEANCE. By FRANK BARRETT.
TWO PINCHES OF SNUFF. By WILLIAM WESTALL.
IN ONE TOWN. By E. DOWNEY.
ANCHOR WATCH YARNS. By E. DOWNEY.
ATLA. By Mrs. J. GREGORY SMITH.
LESS THAN KIN. By J. E. PANTON.
THE NEW RIVER. By SOMERVILLE GIBNEY.
COMEDIES FROM A COUNTRY SIDE. By W. OUTRAM TRISTRAM.

12, YORK STREET, COVENT GARDEN, W.C.

FOR THE COMPLEXION.

BEETHAM'S
GLYCERINE AND CUCUMBER

Is the most perfect Emollient Milk for PRESERVING and BEAUTIFYING the SKIN ever produced! It entirely removes and prevents all ROUGHNESS, REDNESS, SUNBURN, CHAPS, &c., soon renders the SKIN SOFT, SMOOTH, and WHITE, and preserves it from the effects of exposure to the SUN, WIND, FROST, or HARD WATER, &c., more effectually than any other known preparation. No Lady who values her COMPLEXION should ever be without it, as it is INVALUABLE at all Seasons for keeping the SKIN SOFT and BLOOMING. It is perfectly Harmless, and may be applied to the Tenderest Infant. Bottles, 1s., 2s. 6d.; 4s 6d.; any size for 3d. extra. N.B.—Beware of Injurious Imitations. Ask for "BEETHAM'S."

BEETHAM'S FRAGRANT
ROSE LEAF POWDER

Is a perfectly Pure and Harmless Toilet Powder which cannot injure the most tender skin. It is delicately tinted to resemble the beautiful colour of the wild rose, and is strongly recommended to be used with the above wash, as it will greatly aid it in keeping the skin clear and healthy, free it from unpleasant moisture, and impart that Beautiful Bloom to the Complexion which is so much admired. Boxes 1s., free for 1s. 2d. In handsome box, containing two tints and puff, 2s. 6d., free for 3d. extra.

BEETHAM'S
CAPILLARY HAIR FLUID
(Free from Lead, Dye, and all Poisons.)

Is unequalled for Preserving, Strengthening and Beautifying the Hair. It effectually arrests Falling Off and Greyness, Strengthens when Weak or Fine, and wonderfully Improves the Growth. It imparts a Rich Gloss to hair of all shades and keeps it in any desired form during exercise. N.B.—It is made in three shades, "Light," "Dark," and "Extra Dark," the last-named being specially prepared to hide Greyness when the hair has turned in patches or streaks, for which it is strongly recommended. It is not a dye. Bottles 2s. 6d. and 4s. 6d., free for 3d. extra.

BEETHAM'S
FRAGRANT HAIR GROWER

Is a delightfully Refreshing and Strengthening application for the hair, quite free from grease or dye, and, being rather more stimulating than the "Capillary Fluid," is recommended where the hair is falling off very much For baldness, or where the hair has fallen in patches, it has been found marvellously effectual in producing a fresh growth of long glossy hair. It also entirely removes all dandruff, and keeps the skin of the head clean and healthy. Bottles 2s 6d., 4s. 6d., free for 3d. extra.

BEETHAM'S
CORN AND BUNION PLASTER

Is the best remedy yet discovered! It acts like magic in relieving pain and throbbing, and soon cures the worst CORNS and BUNIONS. It is especially useful for reducing ENLARGED GREAT TOE JOINTS, which so mar the symmetry of the feet. Thousands have been cured, some of whom have suffered for fifty years without being able to get relief from any other remedy. A trial of a box is earnestly solicited, as IMMEDIATE RELIEF IS SURE! Boxes 1s. 1½d., of all Chemists, free for 14 stamps.

M. BEETHAM & SON, CHEMISTS, CHELTENHAM.

AN EARLY FROST.

CHAPTER THE FIRST.

THEY had just taken the stag on the outskirts of a Buckinghamshire village, and such an essentially "mixed" field as usually follows Her Majesty's hounds were straggling off homewards. It was early Spring, and the sun going down in a ruddy glow behind some beechwoods, threw long shadows upon the plashy roads, and deeper crimson upon faces already red from that last half-hour's gallop.

Farmer Brown, upon a stout cob he had steered along the roads without attempt at deviation all day walked that animal home-

A

wards beside its very counterpart bestridden by Farmer Harris, in wake of the straggling field.

The two sturdy yeomen, almost as alike as their respective mounts, farming lands that joined and ran into each other with an intricacy above the understanding of any but natives of Fair-acres, made a picture good to look at as they jogged amicably back to their homesteads side by side.

"A fine gallop—uncommon!" Farmer Brown said, pulling out a large watch and looking at the time.

"Uncommon," Farmer Harris replied, with a weatherwise eye turned towards the clear sky

"Is it frost?"

Farmer Harris brought his eye down again and let it rest upon his brother in pitchforks.

"Like enough, ain't it?" he asked.

Farmer Brown took a survey of the cloudless sky himself, critically, and seemed to agree, for he replied with the comprehensive word, "Un-common." Whereupon the two neighbours, keep-ing pace with the straggling field, trotting on when the field trots, dropping back to a walk when the field walks, proceed a couple of miles side by side in silence.

They might have gone the whole way home without further exchange of ideas, but, at the named distance, a girl followed by a groom trotted up from behind and overtook them. She was quite young, not more than seventeen, with a quantity of golden hair twisted up tight under a killing little hat; with a face like an angel's, all pink and white, but so childish and so pure that you instinctively turned your head away, and felt strangely unsuited to associate with such innocence, when she looked at you.

She smiled and nodded to the two yeomen as she passed them, and they returned her greeting almost reverentially.

"Do you see how well she rides the mare Harris? Don't she now?" Brown asks as the slight figure on the fiery black goes on ahead of them.

"Uncommon," replies Harris, using his favourite word.

"Did you see her a-going to-day—like a bird? Did you see that, Harris?"

Still Harris's favourite word is equal to the occasion, and he uses it.

"The question to me is, what can Mrs Bethray be about a-letting her only child out a-hunting and a-what-not-ing, and she allus in London taking no notice of her?"

Harris is silent a moment, perhaps pondering how he can utilise his word, but he gives it up, and says,—

"Mrs Bethray is a widow, Brown. Mrs Bethray, Brown, is a *young* widow. Mrs Bethray, Brown, is not more than thirty-six, I should reckon. May be she (having been a fine looking one to look at—being so still) may not fancy having a grown up daughter about along of her—may be so, Brown."

"May be so, Harris," the other assents placidly, and they jog on a while in silence; then Brown says,—

"You hev reckoned that leetle matter, Harris —reckoned it uncommon, I may say. Do you reckon as there's any truth as our landlord, Mr Darrac, is after this here golden-haired angel in her mother's absence?"

"Ay, and in her mother's presence too, Brown. I reckon as Mrs Bethray would be only too glad to get that child married out of the way, be the man *who* he might."

"But Mr Charles Darrac is so precious poor —the manor and its lands, and *our* lands, as you know well, Harris, was mortgaged knee-deep by Charles Darrac's father. Look how Mr Charles Darrac lives!—two rooms of the manor furnished, and an old woman to cook and do for him. Surely Mrs Bethray wouldn't give her willing consent to them two paupers a-marrying?"

"It's my opinion as Mrs Bethray would give her consent to her daughter a-marrying of a dustman, if so be as he offered. Who is that a-riding alongside her and speaking to her now?"

Brown looked on ahead, and saw a well-mounted, well-looking man enough (if you could get over a little coarseness and sensuality in a fat, clean-shaved face) riding very close to Miss Bethray, and leaning in her direction to speak to her.

"Why, that be Mr Huson," Brown says, completing his scrutiny.

"Who be Mr Huson?"

"One of the London gents as come down by the special—'mazing rich they do say."

"What be Mr Huson?" Harris inquires further.

"That nobody don't know as I can find out. He seems to have took to Miss May. I see him a-speaking to her last Tuesday, and the Friday afore. Depend upon it, Harris, Mrs Bethray will live to rue the day she was always a-neglecting of her daughter. Don't you think so, Harris?"

The opportunity is far too good to be missed. Harris jumps at it.

"Uncommon," he says, shaking his head sagely. "Un-com-*mon*, Brown," he adds, with emphasis, and the two neighbours and friends jog on together to the spot where their paths diverge, without another word.

Meanwhile May Bethray disengages herself from the attentions of Mr Huson, which bore her, and putting Black Diamond into a canter upon some roadside turf, is soon out of sight of the straggling field. The air is fresh with the calm of a coming frost as she enters the long avenue leading to the low, rambling old place known as Fairacre Grange; and there is still crimson on tree and hedgerow, where the blushing glances of the setting sun fall on them. A glorious evening to anybody, but Paradise to one to whom the scents of the earth, and the beauties of the landscape, and the still happiness of home, all mysteriously syllable a name: the name of the man to whom a fresh, untarnished, girlish heart has gone out, with the passion of those days that are only a memory to most of us now!

CHAPTER THE SECOND.

SPRINGING lightly down from Black Diamond at the glass-fitted porchway, May stands a moment with the horse's nose affectionately thrust into her hand, whilst she says softly: "There never *was* another like you, old girl; I would trust my life to you any day"

Black Diamond whinnies a reply, and turns her glossy head, as she is led away, to get one more look at the mistress by whom she has been ridden with such liberality and confidence all day.

An elderly housekeeper meets Miss Bethray in the hall.

"I have a telegram from Mrs Bethray, Miss May," she says, handing it. "She will be home to-morrow by dinner time. Will you have some tea before you change?"

Mrs Mews has acted as housekeeper at the Grange ever since May can remember; a thoroughly good-hearted, motherly old soul, more motherly a thousand times to the only child than Mrs Bethray

"One cup down here, when I *have* changed, thank you, Mews, and then I'll take my usual quick walk before it gets quite dark," and May Bethray flies away upstairs gaily, singing as she goes.

"It's all very well saying she 'leaves her with confidence to me,' the pretty little thing," Mews soliloquises, walking with the solemnity of a portly figure towards her own apartments. "But I'm not altogether capable. I know it; I feel it every moment of the day. If I had such a daughter, I wouldn't leave her to take care of herself. Miss Raffles ought to have stayed another two years at least! Fancy sending away a governess when a young lady gets to be seventeen! Not that Miss Raffles were overmuch use — the old fossil! umph!" and Mrs Mews grunts. There used to be an old feud between governess and housekeeper; but it is dying out in these grunts now.

In less than twenty minutes, May comes out of the glass-fitted front door, in a smart little walking costume, and takes her way down one of the shrubbery walks at a rapid pace; not exactly with the manner of one taking a constitutional; there is too much set purpose about it for that. Pinker, and whiter, than her balmy namesake, she swings quickly along, with firm, well-balanced steps that make the shrubbery path a very short one, and the stile with the holly-bushes each side of it, much nearer than it would seem to you or me; a high stile, with a foot-board to it, leading from the Grange shrubbery to a footpath through one of the Manor plantations; an unfrequented, lonely stile, with wonderful conveniences about it for lounging or sitting. Just the place, is Hollybush stile, for meetings, and confidences, and mutual vows,— all the 'business' in fact, of that great drama of which Cupid is stage manager and prompter all in one.

Gaily May, only pink May now, speeds along the old old road, on the old old errand,—the errand that has worn every road we tread, in every age—the one errand that, with changing centuries and creeds, is alone eternal.

Round this last angle, and she is in view of the stile, within ten yards of it—the prettiest little blushing figure that ever was. The blush dies out for a moment, for she sees no one there, and then flames out again, brighter, deeper, ruddier than before, as she sees that he is playing with her, and has been only hiding behind one of the holly bushes.

"I thought you hadn't taken the trouble to come," she says demurely, looking down, and holding out two little Suède-gloved fingers to him.

Charley Darrac looks at her with a frank, handsome dark face, and exclaims,—

"What! fingers! What on earth is the meaning of this?"

"What do you expect *but* fingers, when you won't do what I ask you? All day I've been galloping about alone, whilst you might have been galloping about with me. It's very shabby of you to spend all your days in that old library, with your musty old books, when you might be out hunting. I don't even call it manly—there."

Charley Darrac leans against his side of the stile, and she, half turning her back upon him, leans against *her* side of it.

"Come, come, Daisy!" the man says, speaking between jest and earnest. "I don't think this is quite fair, is it? You know perfectly well that my old uncle who keeps me going is a confirmed woman hater; that he says if I marry till I can live without his help, he will cut me out of his will altogether. You know that my only chance of *being* able to marry without his help is by hard work. Therefore, don't you see, in reality when I am away from you, studying the musty old books, I am really getting closer to you with every page I turn? Don't you see, Daisy?"

She relents a little as she hears the familiar pet name he alone calls her, and turns a trifle more towards him as she says, still pettishly,—

"What made your terrible old uncle go and get 'crossed in love,' I wonder? And because he is so, why should he hate every woman on earth? I call it abominable of him!"

"But then, remember, please, he hasn't seen *you.*"

"Now, you're absurd, and if you're absurd, I'll put up my umbrella. I tell you distinctly, I will!"

"Well, but, Daisy—"

"If you try to get over this stile, I will put it up that minute!" Miss Bethray exclaims, with a little stamp of her foot, and beginning to unfurl the weapon named.

"I don't know why you carry an umbrella on a clear, frosty evening," Darrac says, laughing. "Are you expecting rain?"

"Never mind what I'm expecting. That's my business. I'm glad to see you keep your own side of the stile."

It was very hard to keep his own side of the stile with that wayward little beauty standing so temptingly on the other; but he was accustomed to humour her caprices, and therefore he went on with a subject he knew would please her.

"What sort of a day have you had? A good day, I suppose, for I saw the hounds going back only half-an-hour ago."

"A very good day—of the sort. We met at the Thicket (do you know that much? I daresay you don't take sufficient interest in the hounds even to look the meets up) and uncarted in Boyne Park. *Such* a gallop across it! The stag took the sunk fence out of it, and the hounds followed, but no one else. Do you know the sunk fence? More than eighteen feet wide, and a bad landing. I had a wild inclination to try Black Diamond at it, but I didn't. Whenever they uncart in Boyne Park, I always *have* a wild inclination to try Black Diamond at that sunk fence. I shall some day. I know I shall!"

"Hush, darling, hush! It would be suicide!" Charles Darrac says, seriously. "No one could get over that alive. I have heard fifty people say so."

"You didn't think I meant it, Charley!" the girl says with a sudden softening of he voice. "You didn't, *really!* You *couldn't* be so silly?

I'm not quite tired of my life yet. When I am, I will try the sunk fence. Does *that* satisfy you?"

"Yes. That is—it would, if I might come over the stile a moment—"

"I'll put the umbrella up if you stir one inch!" Miss Bethray says, turning and facing him with the umbrella pointed towards him, and her hand upon the snap. "One step further, and I fire! It looks like a gun doesn't it?"

"You're *too* bad, Daisy!"

"Too good, you mean, to come out here at all, for that's what I am, and I can't stay a second longer. Good-night! I hope the books will prove interesting to-night. Oh! I say! what a jolly evening you have in store for you!" and she turns away with a ringing, girlish laugh.

The opportunity is not to be missed. Charles Darrac is over the stile at one bound.

"Oh! you terrible fellow! I've a great mind never to come to meet you again!" May exclaims, very red, and, it must be confessed, a little disarranged as to head gear. "And if you attempt to come one step towards home with

me, I'll give you in charge for trespassing, so now
you know"

"Does my lady please that I go straight
home?" her lover asks with mock humility

"Certainly, to the place from whence you
came, there to be hanged—you know! Good-
night once more," and waving a laughing farewell, May Bethray runs off homewards in the
twilight.

The man stood a moment looking after her—
fondly looking after her, his girl love—and then
turned and walked slowly back to the manor and
his musty books. He was very sad. He spoke
bravely enough to May, but in his own heart and
its secrecy, he felt there were long, dreary years
to be travelled before those two lives could
merge into a common existence.

His wealthy uncle had a cast-iron constitution,
and came of a long-lived race. And, as to the
other alternative—the earning sufficient to keep a
wife—who ever heard of a poet doing that? No;
a preacher might, if very eloquent for foreign
missions; a pork butcher might, for there is a
continual demand for pork in this Christian

country ; but a poet ! For such there only existed the probability of a steady descent to the deepest bottom of penury and contumely. How *can* a poet exist in an age that has no heroic deeds to sing ? Heroics went out when mechanics came in. Who could write a sonnet to a sewing machine, or indite an elegy on the electric telegraph ? Why, a poet in this age is about as incongruous as a Ritualistic curate would have been in that of the Cæsars. And yet poor Charles Darrac *was* a poet, and a poet only. Such a man can be nothing else ; and he felt that waiting for the day that should see him able to keep a wife upon rhymes—with or without reason—was a very long wait indeed. But poor little May went singing home blithely, thanking Providence that it was only a paltry lack of gold standing between herself and her love. Only a little gold ! hardly worth mentioning or thinking about, when they both loved each other so ! What a dead-simple problem life is at seventeen !

As May passed the windows of the drawing-room, where a cheery fire made visible the interior, she saw, sitting there, two figures she

B

recognised at once. The Vicar's wife and the
Vicar's daughter had an awkward habit of constantly dropping in at the Grange, especially
when Mrs Bethray was away, and seeing if
May was getting "along all right," as Mrs Marfleet put it.

An expression, half uttered, rose to May's lips
as she saw the unmistakable figures, and it
sounded very like "Oh, bother!"

"I felt it due to your charming mother to
come and see you to-night. You're out rather
late, aren't you?" Mrs Marfleet said, taking May's
plump little hand in her own bony, black-gloved
one.

"I always take a sharp walk after hunting,
Mrs Marfleet; I think it's good for one," May
answered, looking straight into the somewhat
hard and equine face of the Vicar's wife.

"I should really be afraid to be out *alone* so
late," from Miss Marfleet, also equine.

It flashed upon May on the instant that the
fear, under such circumstances, might more
correctly rest with the unlucky individual encountering Miss Marfleet's forbidding exterior.

"Oh! I don't think there's much danger," she said, laughing at the thought. "Mother is coming back to-morrow evening; we have had a wire about it."

"And you are quite well and happy alone here, are you?" questioned Mrs Marfleet.

"Quite well, and very happy. Black Diamond never went better than to-day. I was in front from start to finish—glorious!" and Miss Bethray turned a glowing, enthusiastic face, from equine mother to equine daughter.

There was no response in either of them, only strong righteousness of a pronounced order.

"Will you have some tea?" she asked, stifling a sigh.

In the capacity of sole girl friend May Bethray had, Sarah Marfleet was sadly wanting, and May felt her so—often.

"No tea, thanks; we have had ours long ago We merely came to pay our duty call of inquiry in your charming mother's absence. I wonder you can get on so cheerfully without her," Mrs Marfleet answered.

By judicious donations to coal and blanket

clubs ; by judicious anxiety as to, and support of,
other village charities, the worldly beauty, from
whom Time was taking liberal toll of the latter,
but leaving the former very much intact, had entirely won the heart of Mrs Marfleet, who always
spoke of her as " charming Mrs Bethray."

It was a happy little mutual arrangement, in
fact. Very simple. In effect, charming Mrs
Bethray said : " You support me with any
schemes I may have for the management of
little May — as she only sees you and your
daughter, it will not be difficult to influence her
mind—and *I* will provide you parish funds to
the best of my ability."

Very simple this, and perfectly tacit ; thoroughly well understood notwithstanding. With
such uncongenial surroundings, with only a
cold-hearted, equine-faced, mature young lady
of twenty blank, as sole confidant and associate,
not surprising that the delicate flower, yearning
for something deeper and stronger, should have
thrown its fragrant blossoms over the boundary
fence, and flourished there, fed by the water of
the Eternal Spring !

"Oh! I get on fairly well without mother—she *is* away a good deal," May answered. "But I—I manage, you know. I'm used to being alone, you see."

There was a blush upon the delicate cheek as she spoke, but nobody notices blushes by firelight.

"Very wise, indeed, of your charming mother, I think, keeping you from 'coming out' as long as she can. It has already fostered a taste for the country in you. I'm sure you don't want to go to nasty smoky London, and its silly gaieties. Do you now?"

"Oh, no! I *never* want to go to London unless I am obliged. I hope I never *shall* be obliged."

It was spoken with such a genuine ring of earnestness in the words that Mrs Marfleet looked at her daughter in the dim light with a glance that said plainly,—

"How *very* well charming Mrs Bethray manages things! Hardly another girl in England would live in a quiet country home in preference to London gaieties!" Then she said aloud: " Well, we must be going now. Modred will be wondering where we are."

The Rev. Modred Marfleet made a convenient name for his wife to conjure with when occasion arose. It was the only use he ever was to her. Indeed, he was not much beyond a name to anybody. Profound and continual study of dead languages seemed (without other apparent results) to have taken all that was in any way living out of him. Beyond grammar and hair, there was very little of the Rev. Modred Marfleet.

May Bethray went to the door with her visitors took cordial leave of them there, and then, encountering Mrs Mews in the hall on her return, hugged that old lady with unfeigned affection,—

" Oh! Mews!" she cried, at the highest top sparkle of youthful hilarity " I'm *so* happy and *so* lively, I don't know what to do. Will you race me upstairs now ? "

Upon Mews kindly but firmly declining, the little beauty dashed into the drawing-room, and began thundering off valses with the greatest power at her command, first looking, however, through a certain angle window of the room at a certain other window, with a steady light burning in it, just visible at the distance of a quarter of a mile, through a glade in the surrounding trees: looking straight into Fairyland with that glance!

CHAPTER THE THIRD.

OLD haunts have an irresistible fascination for most people. It doesn't much matter what the associations are ; happy or unhappy, if we have only trod the ground often enough, our heart goes back there, and takes our body with it very frequently. Especially is this true of youthful haunts. It seems almost impossible to believe that, standing on the same spot, breathing the same air, we shall not feel as we used to feel in the old days that were so young! The place you used to meet *her!* you have not forgotten that! It signifies less than nothing what the sequel of those meetings was; sad or gay—laughter or tears—or that fate co-mingling both those emotions in the strangest way—you can't go there to-day without believing some of the old incense you burnt there yet lingers in that unhackneyed air! As that is so with you—a lord of the creation, mighty, giving and taking hard knocks in the great battle of life every day—so, in a modified degree, does the feeling pertain to the heart of woman. In a modified degree, of course. The creature who can appreciate sweetmeats and tea, cannot, in the nature of things, have passion ranking with those of the creature appreciating beefsteaks and brandy. It is absurd to expect it. Yet there is a reflex of this impulse in the heart of "lesser man." It is hard, while parting rays of a beauty that is setting are upon her, for her to forego the scenes of her old triumphs. Charming Mrs Bethray found it especially hard. She tore herself away from town for a while now and then, and patronised local charities in Fairacres; but she came back again sooner or later to the paved streets and the garish lights.

There were certain gaieties at certain houses from which she could not keep away; with the best endeavours, could not. Whenever her old friend Mrs Berkely entertained on a large scale, for the very life of her, Laura Bethray could not absent herself.

It is because Mrs Berkely is giving a dance to-night that Laura is up in town. It is a fine excuse for a week's absence from the country which bores her. If it were not for little May, charming Mrs Bethray would have had a snug little house in London long ago. But, being not altogether a fool, the fact has taken root in charming Mrs Bethray's charming little golden head that a grown up daughter would not tend towards the increase of that homage she can still exact from men — that homage for which she lives. No: little May is very much better, in all lights, down amongst the beechwoods of Fairacres "strengthening her constitution," as her charming mother puts it, with country air!

Not very many troubles worry charming Mrs Bethray; chiefest amongst them is that common one best described, perhaps, as "insufficiency of income;" a trouble which, by-the-way, has brought more people to grief than any other.

If she has further worries, they are that she
is not so young as she was, in the first place,
and that a certain good-looking young military
dandy (a flame that has been in a flickering
state of combustion for the last twenty years
or so) won't come up to the scratch and
propose.

But Roland Vance *won't.* Aggravating man,
he *won't.* She has believed he would at every
gathering at which she has met him; she
believes he really *must* at Mrs Berkely's dance
to-night. She is even more than usually careful to hide Time's milestones as she caparisons
herself for the fray at John's Private Hotel
in George Street, Cavendish Square. A select
little hotel, extremely snug and cosy, is John's
private one in George Street, Cavendish Square.
Charming Mrs Bethray is thoroughly well-
known and understood there, and always uses
it as a consequence.

There is a great awning out at No. Blank
Portman Square by ten o'clock to-night, and a
great banging of carriage doors and champing
of bits as a young sickle moon looks down

from a clear frosty sky a little later. A row of footmen, so tall and straight, and white headed, they might pass for billiard cues, line the hall in an imposing manner as the guests arrive all cloaked and beautiful (of course beautiful), and so struggle slowly up the great staircase to the cloakroom which is at the top of it.

Charming Mrs Bethray has come in and gone upstairs some time (with such a beautiful, delicate blush upon her check as nature never came within a mile of), before a military-looking man, no longer a youth, drives up in a hansom, and endeavours to pay the driver by means of a shilling, and, being unable to effect it, adds an additional sixpence, and accompanies it with such remarkably strong language that the human billiard cues blush under their powder—only a ladiesmaid, chancing to hear, looks at Roland Vance with undisguised admiration, and says what a fine looking, fine made man he is!

Some women are so easily pleased!

Upstairs it is the old scene: hot rooms, perfumed air, a cubic space about half that usually required for comfort allotted to each person; band in an alcove, evidently feeling the heat acutely; weary old chaperons, not a bit enjoying it, and trying to look as though they were; elegantly dressed young men enjoying it immensely, and trying to look as though they weren't; female loveliness of every rank and order. Supposing you have given up "winning beauty" as a bad job, or (may be sadder case) that you have irrevocably won it, all balls are very much alike to you and me, old friend!

Singular how a woman with an object in view can arrange details towards the furthering of that object! If there is a richer man in view—or a worse—a man in any way more interesting to her than you, you may strive all night to get a *tête-à-tête* with her in vain. But if only you are desirable in any way, you'll see her alone in a dimly lighted alcove, or behind a palm tree, or in some other equally tempting situation, every ten minutes the whole evening.

It was in the former of these happy hunting grounds that Roland Vance came upon charming Mrs Bethray, within five minutes of entering Mrs Berkely's ball-room. If he had wanted to avoid her, it would have been difficult, Laura had disposed herself so skilfully. But he didn't appear to wish to avoid her. He went straight up to her at once.

"Why, Laura," he said, "I didn't expect to see you here; I made sure you would have been taking care of Mademoiselle at Fairacres."

"Ah, you never *did* understand anything about *me*," the golden haired, faded beauty answered, with a tone of sadness in her voice. "You never did, Roland."

"Come, that's rather good, Laura, when you went and shunted me in favour of Bethray," Captain Vance replied in an injured tone.

A very pretty sight for gods and men, those two worldly, false, artistically arranged specimens of humanity, playing at simplicity, and love, and injured innocence!

Yet as Laura Bethray looked at the handsome *roué* face of the man, who had seated himself easily upon the seat beside her, just in the way she recollected so well in the old days before the apple was eaten, she saw none of the lines Time had written there with his indelible ink; only the face she remembered young and fresh —her *first* face! And as she so looked, she felt that, so far as she was concerned, the love was rising as strong as ever. Why was it not so with him?

"Do you ever think of those old days?" she asked him, waving her fan softly in her old, graceful way, and speculating whether the action recalled *her* as she used to be to *him*.

"How can I ever forget them, Laura?"

"Don't be conventional and silly, please, Captain Vance. Let us try to be rational."

"I never was more so. Do you remember the old apple-woman at the corner of the square, who used to act as Cupid's postman."

"*How* all your letters smelt of apples, too, Roland!"

"Silly old days, silly old ways, and yet very pleasant ones," the man said musingly.

" It's fearfully sad to think one can never recall such ways and days, Laura ! "

Laura's worldly little heart began to beat perceptibly faster. He had never been *quite* so near as this before !

" I'm sure I don't know it would be impossible, if we tried *very hard indeed,*" she said, very low.

The man, whose eyes had been upon her face, turned them away rapidly, and looked through the draperies screening the alcove, out across the many coloured figures of the ball-room, and saw none of them.

Laura noticed the glance and its abstraction, and believed he was dwelling tenderly upon the old, old days: thought the doubtful look upon his face was the doubt of her heart, not the skilful weighing of chances done by one more than usually cautious in his actions.

A happy couple, together at last, made for the alcove, half drew aside the curtains, saw it was occupied, and left hurriedly with annoyed faces; then Roland Vance brought his eyes back again to Laura's, with a half smile, and said sadly,—

"We might try very hard, no doubt; but you recollect the old spectre that stood between us? He has not grown any less terrible with increased familiarity, Laura. He is very vital still."

She understood him in a moment.

"I don't see we need have any secrets," she said, looking out over the ball-room in her turn. "I have a trifle over two thousand a year—not the capital, you know, but the interest. Most unfortunately, not the capital, which goes to May, or failing her, to Mr Bethray's family when—when I have done with it. But, Roland, don't you think we could manage, you and I, on a couple of thousand a year?"

"*You* spend it all, I suppose, and have done since you've had it?" the man asked carelessly; and then, not heeding her quiet "I'm afraid I do," went on: "But still it could be man aged, I've no doubt, only—only—" and he stopped.

C

" Only *what*, Roland ? No secrets, you know."

"Then, Laura, to be plain with you—to be perfectly open and plain with you—I'm no saint. I've been fearfully extravagant all along. I've debts, pressing debts. If I can't find some way of clearing them off in the next year, they will clear me off. Do you understand ? I shall have to bolt."

" How silly to incur debts, Roland ! "

" Of course, it was silly ; but they're not recent debts, Laura. They are an old legacy of my younger days. If they were once cleared—but it's no good talking, there's no hope of that, and I couldn't drag you into all the bother of them. I couldn't think of it. If I had a good friend now, who would lend me his name—but it's no use talking."

" What good would a *name* do ? "

" Don't you see ? I could borrow sufficient to pay all these debts which are pressing. and re-pay the one loan by instalments. But it's no use talking, for I haven't the friend."

" Shouldn't I do, Roland ? "

"Dearest Laura, of course you'd do, no doubt of it; but I couldn't dream of such a thing—I really couldn't."

"Nonsense! Think what old friends we are! Besides, suppose I said—a fearfully bold thing *to* say" (with a bashful raising of the face) —"suppose I said my happiness depended upon you being clear—after what you have said to-night?"

The draperies of the alcove are fairly thick; there is no wandering couple at hand, for a valse is in dreamy progress. Roland Vance takes the gloved hand upon the lap beside him, kisses it with effusion, and says warmly,—

"Laura, you have made me the happiest of men—the very happiest! How can I ever thank you enough?"

She tells him how he can, in whispers; they exchange vow for vow, there in the alcove, in the same low tone, Time's milestones, in spite of art, very visible the while upon them both—a sight for gods and men! The whole affair has a want, or lack of something—an indefinable something, that robs it of its poetry, and makes it false and stagey. Utterly incomparable with the real thing enacted, four or five hours earlier, that very evening at Hollybush stile!

But, then, we can only have a Hollybush stile *once* in our lives!

CHAPTER THE FOURTH.

In a certain narrow street running out of Piccadilly, in a direction parallel with St James's, and on the same side of the way, a remarkably unassuming brass-plate of small dimensions bore the plain inscription:

Mr HUSON.

First Floor.

The plate itself was not affixed to the outer door, which was blank, but to a second or inner one, opening directly upon the narrow staircase. The first-floor room was very plainly furnished, containing a large writing-table, a safe, three chairs, and a small shelf of books—the library being limited to a Peerage, Baronetage, *Burke's Landed Gentry*, and a Turf Guide; with the

exception of *Whittaker's Almanac*, and a small
carriage clock upon the mantel-shelf, the whole
contents of Mr Huson's first-floor have been
enumerated.   Extremely simple stock-in-trade
wherewith to draw in a very handsome income,
and yet sufficient for that purpose.   Add only
an elderly clerk, with a chronic cough, in a side
room, and you have all Mr John Huson's visible
pecuniary machinery.

Simpler things never worked graver work than
these things did, however.   In combination with
certain raw material (always scrupulously dressed
in the latest fashion), this cheery little machine
ground down paternal acres and noble woods,
even at times family jewels, with amazing cel-
erity and dispatch.

To this pretty little gilded bower came impecunious youth, strong in caligraphy; youth
suffering under tenacious relatives, vigorous in
cash and constitution.   Thither, so far as the
value of them was concerned, came the paternal
acres, sooner or later; and the peculiarity of the
gilded bower was that, though quantities of
gold went out of it, in some mysterious way it

always came back again in twofold volume. In fact, Mr John Huson was a sort of eastern husbandman, casting his bread upon the waters of fashion, and finding it, fructified beyond all imagination, after many days.

Two separate and distinct personalities were combined in that of John Huson. There was the John Huson of the Queen's Hounds, jovial, open-handed (to a certain extent), riding pretty straight, and enjoying it; and there was the John Huson of that first-floor room, keen, prompt, serious, with a bull-dog grip, when he once laid hold, immovable as Gibraltar. His enemies said there was even a third John Huson, kept very much in the dark indeed: a champagne supper-eating, two o'clock in the morning John Huson; but, as he was a bachelor, that was essentially his own affair, and nobody else's.

John Huson usually drove up to his office, behind a smart horse, from his house down St George's Square way, about eleven o'clock every morning but hunting mornings. As a matter of fact, business with him seldom began till past twelve, but the hour was useful for letter writing and reading the *Times*, a copy of which, duly cut by the elderly clerk with the chronic cough, lay daily upon his writing-table on his arrival.

Driving up to-day as usual, John Huson goes up the narrow stairway, enters his room, hangs his hat on a peg in the clerk's department, and his overcoat along with it, and then, without a word to his subordinate, sits down to his table and his letters.

Having read through some half-dozen, he takes up a pen and writes a few on his own account. Fateful epistles for the most part—appetite destroying epistles—for many a bold soldiering heart turns sick at the sight of John Huson's clear, business-like handwriting.

He has soon done, and takes up the newspaper; has read systematically through births, deaths and marriages (all three of which headings have a professional interest for him, and of some of which he takes a note), when the clerk opens the partition door and announces "Mrs Bethray."

It would seem charming Mrs Bethray is there
by appointment, for John Huson looks at his
watch on receiving the intelligence, and then
says : "Show her in."

He gives her a chair when she enters the
room, a chair opposite his, and facing the light,
though she makes a feeble attempt to take one
with a contrary direction.

"Mrs Bethray, you are punctuality itself," he
says pleasantly, seating himself.

Mrs Bethray murmurs something about "hoping
so." The fact is plainly evident that charming
Mrs Bethray is rather flurried and nervous in
the present situation. The white, rather coarse,
clean-shaved face opposite her, with cold, grey
eyes fixed closely upon hers, does not tend toward setting her at her ease. Huson notices this,
and not appearing to, goes on at once,—

"Well, to get to business. Captain Vance, as
no doubt you know, requires a loan of three
thousand pounds. He wanted me to do it upon
his own security alone, and I declined. I wanted
another name. Merely a matter of form, but
still necessary. After some delay, he mentioned

you as being willing to give that name. To save you trouble and unpleasantness, he gave me particulars of your position, which I have since verified. We always verify, you know; a mere matter of form, but we always do it."

He pauses a moment, and charming Mrs Bethray, looking terribly faded in the full face of day, says nothing, merely bows, and Huson goes on.

"Mrs Bethray, I may tell you at once that your name is no use to me in this matter—no use at all. You have an income, true; but you have nothing else. The capital of that income you cannot touch; you see, I know all about you."

Truly he did! A great deal more about her, and her character too, than she had any idea of. He had made her character a study for some time, and though he had never spoken to her before, he knew her thoroughly.

"I am very sorry to hear this, for Captain Vance's sake," she said feebly.

She felt it meant farewell to Roland and her highest hopes.

As you may see a steersman at the wheel cast his eye critically aloft, and put his rudder over in exact accordance with what he sees there, so now John Huson, with his eyes intent upon Laura Bethray's face, and reading it, chose his words in accordance with what that face told him.

"As I understand it, you are very anxious— for Captain Vance's sake—that this advance should be carried out?"

"Extremely anxious, Mr Huson."

"As you are a friend of his, I am not surprised at that. It is within my general knowledge that, unless it *is* arranged, the Captain will shortly be in great trouble—more shortly than he thinks."

The shot tells.

"Oh, *can* you not oblige us—oblige *me?*" Laura says, with a ghost of her old set glance that used to be so efficacious.

Still steering his course by her face, and feeling his way carefully, Huson replies,—

"I am going to surprise you, Mrs Bethray; I am going to say something that you've no idea of. I am going to tell you a way in which it *can* be done."

"Yes!" she exclaims eagerly; "what is it? I am willing to do anything."

"Do you mean that, Mrs Bethray?"

"Most earnestly I mean it, Mr Huson."

"Then the matter will not be difficult. I know your part of the country very well; I am a constant follower of 'The Queen's.' Out with them, I have had the pleasure of making the acquaintance" (eyes very searchingly fixed here) "of your daughter, Mrs Bethray."

"Yes," quite cheerily.

"With your daughter, Mrs Bethray, lies the solution of this difficulty."

"I—I think—I understand you," Laura says faintly.

It does not seem such an easy affair, on second thoughts.

"Of course you understand me, Mrs Bethray! We are people of the world, I see that. It is far better for us both to be frank. I have seen a great deal of your daughter. I am a single man, with a sufficient income. Do you give your consent?"

Charming Mrs Bethray is not silent long. It is very little matter to her who marries the child, so long as he is rich, and can keep her comfortably, and, above all, *take her out of the way.*

"It seems strange, on such a short acquaintance, doesn't it?" she asks, trying to appear wavering, and failing miserably. "She is very young, you know, *very* young. And then, too, I can't answer for her heart; I can't *make* her marry you, you know."

But she said it as if she would make her if she could; said it so plainly, that John Huson could not help exclaiming, "Oh! you brute!" between his teeth, knowing as he *did* know the *reason* that made the pale, faded piece of in-anity before him so willing to sell her daughter to the first bidder.

"You cannot make her, of course," he answered, smothering the exclamation; "but she is very young, as you say. You can *influence* her, Mrs Bethray."

"Whatever I *can* do in that way, I will do rely upon me."

"It will be strange if, both together, we cannot bring her to our views," Huson said, in the
business-like tone he would have discussed an
advance in the ordinary daily routine. "I am
sure you have influence with your daughter, Mrs
Bethray."

"Undoubtedly I have; but I tell you frankly,
Mr Huson, she has a wonderful will—her father
had the same. Still, she is very tender-hearted,
poor little thing. I think, if there should be
any difficulty—though I don't see in the least
why there should be" (with a complimentary
glance at the money-lender) — "I think that,
even then, I know a way by which I could
make her do as I wished."

Huson bowed. There was something infinitely
disgusting, even to his dulled senses of honour
and propriety, in this heartless talk, this rely-
ing on a daughter's love for her mother for the
effecting that daughter's sale. He was silent
a moment, and then he said,—

"I am a business man, Mrs Bethray. Therefore, before we go any further, let us thoroughly
well understand each other. I am willing, on one

condition, to do what no other financial agent in London would do—I am willing to advance the Captain three thousand pounds upon the merely nominal security of his own name and yours. The Captain makes a doubtful income on the turf—has nothing beyond that — a bad season there would finish him altogether. Your security is (pardon me, in the way of business) scarcely more valuable, from my point of view. Still, I am willing to make the advance on the condition before mentioned, and that is, that your daughter will become my wife. The day she marries me, Captain Vance has his three thousand pounds. Is that clearly understood?"

" The day she *marries* you, Mr Huson?"

Mr Huson laughed quietly.

"Oh! not before," he said pleasantly. "I am a business man, Mrs Bethray, and a business man only. When did you think I should make the advance?"

"I thought, perhaps—I didn't know, of course —but I thought, perhaps, the day she accepted you."

"Acceptance and marriage are two separate things, Mrs Bethray. There *is* such a thing as breaking off an engagement. I am a business man, you see."

"Oh! *I* am quite willing. After what you have said, it really seems very liberal of you to make the advance at all. But remember how young she is, Mr Huson! You would not expect her to marry you very soon?"

"I'm afraid I should, if the thing is to be done at all. Three months hence would not be too soon. Remember, I know Miss Bethray very well; have done so for some time. Remember also that, if any good is to be done Captain Vance, it must be done soon."

He read her as easily as you read the news bill of a daily, with the electric light upon it. Captain Vance might alter his mind as to her if there were any great delay.

"I have said I will support you in the matter, and I will; but it *does* seem rather soon," she said.

Inwardly she was pleased, though. The horizon was cleared so much quicker than she could have hoped.

"Thank you, Mrs Bethray," Huson said as she rose to go. "You may rely upon me."

She shook hands quite cordially with him on parting, turned back at the door, and said gaily,—

"As it is to be such a short engagement, you had better lose no more time than is necessary. I was going down to Fairacres some days ago, but I wired my change of plans; I am going down to-day, however—will you come down to-morrow and stay till Monday?"

Huson looked at her with a strange expression on his face, and then thanked her, and said he would.

"She would have made an excellent Brahmin priestess," he said to himself as she went out.

CHAPTER THE FIFTH.

IT made no very deep impression upon May when she learnt by telegram that her mother's return to Fairacres was postponed a day or two. She was accustomed to being left alone down there, and had formed her own amusements in consequence. She had no idea she had been taken into the market and sold, like a bale of silk or a cargo of grain. She screwed the telegram up into a ball, and pelted Mews with it, laughing immoderately all the time.

"I suppose it's because I'm young that I feel so happy, and so full of spirits," she said. The next instant: "Oh! what a horrible nuisance to think we all have to get old, Mews! Only

fancy a day when one doesn't care for chocolate
and frosted violets! It is not worth living for,
is it?"

Mews didn't believe, looking wonderfully affectionately at the golden vision before her as she
said so, that Miss May would be anything but
cheerful, and full of life, if she lived to a
hundred.

"Oh, yes, I shall, Mews, with my teeth
falling out, and false hair, and a general
horribleness about me, I've no doubt! *Isn't*
it nasty to think of? Fancy eating with your
gums! I daresay I'll live to be ninety, and
horrid!"

"You'll still be cheerful, Miss May," Mews
persisted.

May looked up from her breakfast (the dia-
logue took place at breakfast time), and made a
most indefensible face at Mews standing beside
the table.

"I'm not very cheerful now, *at rare intervals,*"
she said a shade more seriously, "when I
think that I've no girl friend but Sarah
Marfleet, who's a funny sort of girl, you'll

allow, Mews—funny, you know, without being droll. You understand?"

As the pretty childish face is turned towards her, Mews involuntarily compares it with the bunch of hothouse flowers on the table, and thinks how much sweeter and fairer it is than they are.

"Miss Marfleet is a trifle staid, Miss May, certainly. A bit *staid*, I should call it."

"Mews, you've been young, haven't you? Well, but you've never been a *man*, have you?"

"Oh, Lord! no, miss! What *do* you mean?"

"Ah, of course you haven't—no. But it seems so strange to fancy you young and—slim, perhaps—that I felt, if you had been *that*, you might have been almost anything, you know. I was going to say—I'll put it this way—supposing you *were* a man, Mews, I don't suppose you would be likely to fall in love with Sarah Marfleet? Do you? I don't suppose *any* man would!"

Poor old Mews couldn't bring herself to fancy being a man by any process of reasoning; but agreed heartily with the latter part of the question not understanding it all in the least.

God bless her! how should she? Who could have told her that Sarah Marfleet had said, in May's hearing, that in her opinion Charley Darrac had "lovely eyes that went to anybody's soul," and that in the passionate love of the wayward little beauty's heart had sprung up a foolish, girlish, amazing jealousy? Such wild things or thoughts don't enter the mature heads of half a century! But it was only a passing affair, nothing at all. It vanished at Mews's words for ever, a mere evanescent foam flake on the river of love—the river that runs so swift at seventeen.

Ten minutes later, Black Diamond was ordered for a quiet ride through the leafless lanes, and May was singing gaily at the piano in the drawing-room, in all the happiness of those days that so soon pass away and are gone.

When she came in from her ride, all flushed and rosy with it, Sarah Marfleet was waiting to take her back to the Vicarage to luncheon.

"You're all alone, you know, and you really must come," Sarah said.

There was nothing particularly fascinating in the prospect of such a luncheon. Mrs Marfleet could not be called engaging: Sarah was, to say the least of it, heavy; and the Rev. Modred, well, the simple fact alone that he was one of those men resembling Esau in the matter of hairiness, disposed of *him*. Not content with wearing a beard of patriarchal dimensions, he encouraged hair in all sorts of unusual places— upon the backs of his hands, very likely upon the soles of his feet, to say nothing of small tufts that sprung out of his ears—essentially a hairy man was the Rev. Modred.

But May went to the Vicarage, nevertheless; was wonderfully cheerful there despite the solemn surroundings; but she wouldn't really stay to tea, thanks! No. There were some letters she really *must* write before post time—one being to her mother. She really would go now, thank Mrs Marfleet very much.

Mrs Marfleet—all the Marfleets—were strict

exponents of the Law—the Law that killeth, be it understood, and no other. To write to charming Mrs Bethray was a duty. No further objection was made to May's departure.

There was a brilliant little silver brook that came shooting out of the bank just beside Hollybush stile, and fell into a tiny rivulet passing beside the stile, and parallel with it, under a rustic bridge. But the bridge, on the side the brook fell, was not so wide as the stile, and any one standing on the Grange side of it and looking down, saw a watery mirror there. A clear, ever moving mirror, that all day long reflected waving trees and holly bushes, and the red berries on them, faithfully. All day long there have been mirrored, down below the stile, bare grey branches, bright green holly leaves, and crimson berries, at which the thrushes and the blackbirds have come and sung, and taken toll; and this has made the prettiest of pictures in the watery mirror. But, towards five o'clock, has come the sweetest picture of the day; a blushing, golden picture, with bright blue eyes, and May stands leaning against the stile, looking down. Not for long. The picture has been little more than an instantaneous one, and then it is destroyed as the face is raised—happy, glowing, mischievous—in response to a footfall close at hand.

Well, such pictures never *do* last long!

" What's the use of being a Poet if you can't keep time ?" May asks, but giving him her whole hand (what a little one it is!) to-day

" Keep time, Daisy! You talk of me like a railway train!"

" So you are! Express straight through to Par—Par—Par—what is it ? "

" Parnassus ? "

" That's it! Do the rhymes come all right to-day? By-the-way, what other rhyme is there for sorrow besides 'borrow' and 'tomorrow?' Can you think of one ? "

" I wouldn't think of providing you with rhymes for such an unpleasant word," Charley Darrac answers, laughing.

" That's because you can't think of any more!

I know you! You're a humbug, there! And as to sorrow, I *am* sad to-night. While I was waiting here, I fancied the falling of the little brook there sounded like tears. There's poetry for you! I know it's poetry, it's such non-sense, because, of course, you never can *hear* tears! I wonder what put it into my head?"

A blackbird with a particularly golden bill came and perched upon a neighbouring branch, and looked doubtfully from the lovers to the berries on the holly tree close beside them. Something he saw in those faces assured him they meant no mischief, at least to *him*, and, with a sudden sweep and flutter, he caught a crimson berry and darted off triumphant.

"How can an express train bound straight through to Parnassus tell what put a silly little thought into your head?" Darrac asks, laughing.

"We'll be serious now a moment, if you please—Poet."

"Serious as judges."

"Mother's not coming back till the day after to-morrow."

"Grave and solemn consideration!"

"I'm going with 'The Queen's' to-morrow."

"Almost as solemn a fact."

"I may get killed, and mutilated past recognition."

"Don't be so horrible, Daisy!" the man says, serious in a moment. "Only think what my life would be without you! It would be unbearable."

"You would have your rhymes, you know"

"If you talk like that, I'll come over the stile!"

"Then I'll go home that instant! Indeed, now I think of it, I'll go home as it is. Good-bye!"

She holds out her hand again, and he takes it—from the other side the stile.

"Now!" he exclaims gaily. "I won't let you go unless you give me something!"

"What do you want—a holly berry? (picking one, and holding it up with her disengaged hand).

" No."

" Well, what *do* you want—my glove ? You'll have it soon, in any case, if you pull like that."

" Neither holly berry nor glove ; stoop over here, and I'll whisper."

She doesn't stoop ; she looks at him and laughs.

" I say," she says, " has it ever struck you that these meetings here are awfully silly affairs ? We don't say much, and we don't *do* much, and we only tease each other, has that occurred to you, *Poet ?* "

" It has occurred to me that I couldn't live without them. No ! it's no use struggling. I won't let you go till you give me what I ask."

" What you *haven't* asked yet, you mean," May says, laughing.

" Stoop this way, then, and I will."

" Oh ! look how low the sun is, Charley ! Come, let me go," she pleads.

" Not till you make me that present."

" Charley, fancy how we shall look back on

all this some day! Sha'n't we? And I'm certain
then, when you're old and grey, and, I daresay,
a horrid laureate, or something of that sort, I'm
sure, then, you'll feel terribly ashamed of having held me by the hand and refused to let
me go unless I gave you something! Think
now! *won't* you?"

"Certainly not; it will be the proudest
recollection of my life."

"Well, I shall always be recalling it when
you're getting tired of me, I know I shall!
throwing it in your teeth with fearful per-
sistency. Charles (I shall, of course, have to call
a laureate 'Charles'), Charles, it's all very well
not wishing to take me out with you to-day,
but don't you recollect that day when you
held my hand across Hollybush stile, and
wouldn't let me go unless I gave you something? That will annoy you awfully. Come,
let me go!"

"Not without the condition."

"But perhaps we sha'n't be together at
all! Perhaps you will be 'Lord Darrac of
Fairacres,' and I shall be—dead and buried

in obscurity. There! I'll say something more melancholy if you don't let me go!" She speaks very gaily, but suddenly changing her tone, adds quite seriously: "But, Charley, if it were so, if we *were* parted, I know you'd always remember me *happily*, not sadly —would you? If we were parted, you know?"

"Lean this way, and I'll whisper a reply."

She sees he is obdurate, and so leans towards him for an instant, gives him a little fleeting fairy kiss, snatches away her hand, and darts off homewards, very red and very happy.

Charley Darrac goes homewards too, but seriously. He is wishing he could see his way clearer and more distinctly. Even to a poet two and two won't make five, at least they won't if he is *outside* Hanwell.

So Hollybush stile is deserted, and the brook falls plashing through the bank, and the mirror down below reflects the old picture of bare grey branches and gleaming holly; and the birds come boldly and take the berries,

as they did a hundred years ago, as they will
a hundred years hence, when the lovers shall
have met there for the last time. The last
last time!

CHAPTER THE SIXTH.

"Do *please* be careful, May! See how you've crushed my bonnet!"

Mrs Bethray's greeting to her daughter, who has flung her arms about her mother's neck, and hugged her with all the warm enthusiasm of seventeen.

"But you looked so sweet, you know, coming in at the old door, I really forgot the bonnet and its crushableness," May answers, with a douche-bath feeling upon her.

"Did I look rather well?" (relenting a little at the compliment). "Do these colours harmonise nicely? You've not seen this gown before, have you?"

"No. It's charming! You *do* look well, mother!"

"You've had luncheon, of course, May, long

ago? No — waited? Well, that's very good of you. I'll take these things off, and then have some with you. It's past three o'clock. I'm fearfully tired and hungry."

Sitting at table ten minutes later, with her bonnet off, charming Mrs Bethray doesn't look quite so young. The railway journey, though only a short one, has brought out a whole host of milestones that a gauzy veil was thick enough to hide.

"Well, May, how have you been getting along down here? Hunting, you told me in your letters regularly. No spills, I suppose?"

"Black Diamond never falls—doesn't know how," May says proudly. "I've generally been pretty well in front all day; and once I pounded the whole field; and once—last Tuesday week—"

The girl, with a glowing face, is in full swing with her happy recollections of past sport, when her mother brings her to a sudden check by saying coldly,—

"You hunting people are all alike! You think because you like getting splashed and dirty, and rushing about madly over fences, that everybody likes to hear all your desperate doings in detail afterwards. I daresay it's intensely exciting to *you*—every detail; but please remember I'm no sportswoman, May. How is Mrs Marfleet?"

"I'm very sorry, mother! I forgot it's all nothing to you. Mrs Marfleet is very well. They have been here—Sarah and she — and I have been to the Vicarage more than once since you left."

Silence for a moment, May looking out at the twilight landscape—looking once from it to the clock upon the mantelpiece, with thoughts of the silver mirror and the red berries of Holly-bush stile; Mrs Bethray thinking of that alcove at Mrs Berkely's, and the best way of breaking the news of John Huson's visit to May.

Coming down in the train just now, the same thoughts were in her mind, and they gave her such a pensive expression as she looked out abstractedly at the flying landscape, that an impressionable young gentleman, travelling

E

in the same carriage with her, inwardly
compared her face to that of the Madonna,
and felt romantic. While he was looking
at her from time to time over his *Punch*,
and feeling a profound pity for her sadness
in his heart, charming Mrs Bethray revolved
several taking little lies appropriate to the
deceiving of her daughter in the matter of John
Huson.

Thinking over the best of them now, between picturesque little mouthfuls of cold
chicken, her plan of action takes the following
form:

"Dear me!" (with great surprise and hilarity)
"really, May, I nearly forgot it! We have a
visitor coming down to-morrow to stay till
Monday—a visitor you know."

"Who is it, mother?"

"Oh! you must guess! Somebody I find
you know very well.—Come guess! Sly girl to
keep it to yourself, too. And I only found it
out by accident! Oh! shocking!" and charming
Mrs Bethray shakes a reproving finger at her
daughter.

May blushes in spite of herself. It is so easy to blush at seventeen.

"How can I tell, mother?" she says, laughing. "One knows so many people out hunting, you know. I suppose it isn't Lord Cork, or Frank Goodall?"

"It's all very well to laugh it off, but I see you're blushing," Mrs Bethray says gaily. "It isn't either of those, however. A very good-looking man, just a *trifle* too stout perhaps, but awfully jolly—it's John Huson."

May bursts out laughing.

"*That* old duffer!" she exclaims, greatly amused. "Why, he's a terrible nuisance; he's always trying to talk to me. I've given him cold shoulders enough to feed a regiment; but it's no use, he *will* speak. How on earth did *you* come to meet him?"

Scarcely a hesitation to be called such, and then,—

"In society, dear. He's very well received, you know, because he's so rich—*fearfully* rich, my dear. All the girls in London are after him."

"What! is he single? I should have thought

him married, with forty children!" May laughs gaily.

"Really, dear, how terribly boisterous you are! I'm sure Mr Huson is not more than thirty-eight or nine."

"Ah! but I say, mother, he has—well—run to seed, as *I* should say; lost his figure, as *you* would put it, eh? You can't deny *that*, can you?"

"Don't be so dreadful, May. He's a charming man in society."

"More than he is out hunting, then. Haven't you brought down some especially heavenly sweets, mother? Do you mean to sit there and tell me you haven't?"

"You *must* get out of being a child, really, May. It's so silly to go on as you do at your age, you know. Look at Sarah Marfleet—*study* Sarah Marfleet—May, it will be good for you."

"And like all good things, fearfully trying. Poor old Sal is very *sawdusty*, *I* think. Haven't *you* found her *sawdusty*, mother?"

May turns such an impudent, laughing face towards Mrs Bethray, that Mrs Bethray is

obliged to laugh too. "I shall never do anything with you, May," she says, between annoyance and amusement. "Never."

"We've sat here a pretty good time, haven't
we?" May asks quite innocently, and rising,
as she suddenly catches sight of the moon above
a lime tree. "Now I don't suppose you feel
inclined for the *very sweetest* walk, do you,
mother—just round the shrubberies, you know?"

Sly, mischievous, naughty little May. The
very sweetest walk indeed! Questionable if it
would be so to her if that half invitation to
charming Mrs Bethray were accepted.

"Walk, my dear, when the dews are rising?
I wouldn't think of it. Don't you either; you'll
get a chill."

"I'll chance that, mother; a walk gives me
an appetite for dinner," and Miss Bethray,
laughing a good deal more than the occasion
seems to account for, rushes away to put on
her hat. At the door she pauses a moment
however, and looks back. "Mother, what is old
stick-in-the-mud—Huson? What does he *do*, I
mean?"

" My dear, he is a financier."

" What's that, mother ? "

" Have you heard of the Rothschilds and the Barings, May ? "

" Oh, yes, often."

" Mr Huson, my dear—I don't understand business exactly—he is something of that sort," Mrs Bethray answers airily; and May runs upstairs, singing.

The twilight air seems wonderfully fresh as May hurries down the familiar shrubbery path this evening ; fresher, perhaps, by contrast with charming Mrs Bethray's scents and essences, which always make the air thick and odorous around her. Prettiest sight imaginable this bright blossom of the fairest stem in Nature's garden, stepping lightly along among the leafless branches to meet her lover, in all the innocence of seventeen ; this luxurious branch of Earth's fairest tree, so naturally straying over the boundary fence, to bloom the fresher in Earth's brightest sunshine !

He is there, beside the silver mirror and the falling brook, to-day, waiting for her.

"Well, what's it going to be, Daisy? Fingers, or hands, or—

"Neither fingers, nor hands, nor—*certainly* not anything else! Nothing at all, in fact—Poet."

"What is the matter, Daisy?"

"A sprained wrist is the matter, through some horrible he-creature pulling it so dreadfully last night. That's what's the matter—Poet."

She stands resolutely her side the stile, and a little distance from it, looking at him with a mischievous smile upon her face.

"But we must be friends to-day, Daisy."

"Must we—why?"

"Because it's our last meeting here for a little time—a little time that will seem a very long time to *me*."

"Oh, Charley, what *is* the matter?" the girl asks, coming close up to the stile, serious in a moment, and laying a little hand upon his arm across it, forgetting everything as she stands so, save that they are going to be parted.

"My uncle has written for me to go down into Devonshire to him. I don't know why. He wishes me to go at once : writes most peremptorily about it. I am going up to London to-night, and down by the first train in the morning. You know I am greatly in his hands—I cannot offend him Daisy. But I hate going. I can't bear to leave you only for a short visit. You know that, Daisy?"

"How I do hate *all* these horrible he-creatures!" May exclaims pettishly. "Every one of them!"

"*Every* one, Daisy?"

"Did I make any exception?"

"It's because you didn't, I put the question."

"What exception do you want made?" Miss Bethray asks, back from the stile again now, and defiant once more.

"I wanted you to except *me*."

"But" (laughing immoderately)—"but you *don't* think I included you at all, do you? You're not vain enough to think I included *you*, are you? I meant *men*. I don't call you a man at all, only a—Poet!" (with great disdain).

She stands there laughing at his disgust and mock annoyance, making a wonderfully pretty picture so—a picture that is to be with him constantly in the future, unbanishable.

" You're utterly heartless, Daisy," he says, looking at her with eyes full of admiration.

"Well, who knows but that I've lost it to the he-creature who is coming here to-morrow ? " she asks, teasing him. "A *real* he-creature, you know, worthy the name—no fancy about him—not the least bit of a—Poet."

She always makes a little pause before that noun, and speaks it with terrific energy and distinctness.

" Who is it, Daisy ? "

" What's that to you ? Ask your uncle."

"Tell me at once, or I'll come over the stile ! "

"Oh, I'll tell you, if you're so absurdly anxious about it. This particular he-creature is Mr Huson of London, and he's a financier— the same sort of thing as the Rothschilds and Barings—there ! Does *that* satisfy you ? "

" Thoroughly. I imagine him intensely interesting. You've added the pang of jealousy to the pang of separation."

Perhaps she thinks she has teased him long enough ; perhaps she is really sorry for his going away. She goes up close to the stile again, with a soft hand laid affectionately upon his arm once more.

" Poor old Charley ! I'm _so_ sorry you're going. I shall be _so_ lonely without you ! I shall come here to this stile, at this time, every day, and think about you. I daresay I shall cry—I'm half inclined to now—look there !" and she holds up one of the little Suède-gloved hands, with a sparkling something on it that vanishes while he looks.

He takes that little Suède-gloved hand in his, and kisses it, and she lets him, without a protest, and another little diamond falls somewhere upon her hand or his—it is such an April world at seventeen !

" Darling, will you _really_ be sorry to lose me ?"

"I shall, _really and truly_, Charley—most miserably sorry to lose you; and I'm ashamed of it, and can't think why I tell you of it, and didn't mean to on any account, only—only—I couldn't help it!"

She looks up at him so pitifully, with the tears in her eyes, that he wouldn't have been mortal if he hadn't stooped down and kissed her.

"Never mind, Daisy; it's only for a little while—and then, think! we shall have all our future lives to be together in!"

"Yes, it's all very well, but the future isn't the present, Charley; and just as I was beginning to like you the least little bit! It's *too* bad of your terrible old uncle! It is, indeed. I hope he's got gout, and asthma, and cramp, and toothache, and everything that's horrid!"

"What a fearful complication! But, I say, Daisy, think of the future, when we're old married people, sitting down to tea at this time, you know, most probably, cosily, over the fire —you pouring out, of course."

"I often think of that, that is—no I don't mean that—but—if we do get to that stage, I won't put any sugar in your tea if you go away and don't take me with you—*there!*"

"We will do whatever you like in everything, Daisy, then; you shall be sole mistress.'"

"And we won't have any visitors at all, Charley. Not one, will we? Certainly no *girls* —you know they're so silly, aren't they? We'll live *quite alone,* you and I. Oh! *won't* it be jolly!"

So they spun their webs, those two, with the twilight deepening unheeded around them— twilight that gave shadowy and unreal forms to the material forms about them, but an unreality not half so false as that their own hearts, and their own fancies, gave those objects in the broadest sunshine.

"Charley, see how dark it's getting! I *must* go home, I really must. Mother is at home now, you know; she will be wondering where I am. Must you *really* take the trouble to get over the stile?"

Getting over, and standing a moment with his arm about her waist, Charley Darrac says seriously,—

"If I write to you, you'll answer it, of course ? Will you, Daisy ? "

"But I'm not at all sure you *ought* to write, Charley. I don't know what mother will say if she knows. Well, if you *must*, then, it is only to be once, when you can tell me the day of your return. Don't risk any more letters than that. Don't get me into disgrace, Charley."

"Of course, I won't, darling! Only one letter, and that when I can name the date of my return. Very well, I understand. Let me come to the windows with you, it's so dark!"

"Well, as you're going away, I suppose I must—to within *sight* of the windows, that is. No, there's not room to walk like this; you must follow me, or go on in front. Oh, what nonsense! You will scratch your face, or mine, against the shrubs."

Not a particularly long arm that of Charley Darrac's, but he somehow gets it round all the world while he walks those few hundred yards through the shrubbery.

When she leaves him at last, he stands still,

looking after her as she goes up to the house, in the full glow of the windows of it. The magician's wand has lost none of its potency to-day

CHAPTER THE SEVENTH.

JOHN HUSON travelling down to Fairacres Grange in a roomy first-class smoking-carriage, wiling the hour's journey with a large and choice cigar, smiled to himself more than once over his newspaper. As that paper chanced to be *The Money Market Review*, it is only a natural sequence of ideas which suggests that the reason of those smiles lay outside and beyond that periodical—a correct sequence, too. A little note had come to him that morning with the Fairacres postmark upon it.—

"MY DEAR MR HUSON,—May has somehow got hold of the idea that I met you in society whilst in London. Thinking this a happy mistake of hers, I have not set her right.

Of course I haven't. You understand.—Very
sincerely yours,   LAURA BETHRAY."

Charming Mrs Bethray thought herself uncommonly sharp as she wrote that letter (whilst
May was in Paradise at Hollybush stile) the
preceding night. It looked so much better that
John Huson should imagine the mistake was
May's, and not a cunning lie of her mother's.
But charming Mrs Bethray forgot entirely that
John Huson was a man of the world, and a
remarkably sharp one too. She forgot that
he read her like a book ; that to him, on receiving that note, it was much clearer than crystal
that charming Mrs Bethray had lied to her
daughter with an object, and then tried to deceive him by another lie afterwards. It was
the transparency of the whole proceeding that
made him laugh, even over the pages of *The
Money Market Review.*

There was a neat little single-horsed brougham
waiting for him at Fairacres Station, and he
was soon driving up the Grange avenue, with
an hour in hand before dinner

Mrs Bethray was in the loungy old hall beside a cheery fire burning in the grate there, and welcomed him effusively,—

"I'm afraid you found it cold travelling? No? Yes, it is a cosy old house this, but terribly in the country you know—terribly! I'm not very fond of the country, Mr Huson. No. So much vegetation, I always think, in the country—not at this time of the year, of course, but later and earlier—you know what I mean, don't you?"

A neat servant had meanwhile divested the financier of his overcoat, and he stood forth. in the subdued lamp-light, not a bad-looking fellow by any means, if his jaw had not been quite so heavy, and his nose not quite so thick —not quite such a bull-dog look about him altogether. He was carefully and well dressed, but not *too* well. The art with which he stopped just short of being a mere tailor's model would have passed him as a gentleman, so far as appearance went. There was some tea upon a neighbouring table, and Mrs Bethray pressed her guest to have some of it. But he would not.

F

"Then I'm really afraid I must be running away." the hostess said, with a winning smile. "We have the Vicar's wife and daughter dining here to-night. The Vicar was coming, but has excused himself. Mr Marfleet is a great student—very learned, indeed, you know."

John Hüson made some suitable reply, but his eyes went round the hall with an inquiring glance, and Mrs Bethray interpreted it.

"May will be in before long. She's very young, you know, Mr Huson. She always takes a run through the shrubberies before dinner— to get an appetite, she says. Look here, this is the library, where everybody wanting to smoke *does* smoke. Marchmont will show you your room whenever you wish, if you will just ring the bell. I've no doubt you're dying for a cigar now—do have it here."

" You're very good—if it's really a custom to smoke here. Thank you very much—then, I will."

She assures him that it *is* a custom, and goes out, leaving him there, with another smile bestowed upon him as a parting civility. It is in charming Mrs Bethray's mind that her policy is one of especial correctness towards John Huson.

As for John Huson himself, he smoked a small cigar, with an amused expression on his face, and went off to dress.

When he came downstairs again, and entered the drawing-room, charming Mrs Bethray was standing by the fire, in a black, beaded gown that suited her, and contrasted in a complimentary way with neck and arms that were still white—not what they had been, neither what they would become.

John Huson hadn't advanced to where she stood, hadn't spoken a word to her, when the door was opened again, and May herself came in.

Simple white muslin and a yard or two of blue ribbon don't look very bewitching on a score of women and girls you or I could name at the instant; but on May Bethray, golden May Bethray, you wouldn't have wished for anything more fresh and captivating and pretty.

"This is Mr Huson, my dear," her mother said, watching her face closely the while.

" Well, Mr Huson," May said, looking critically at him, and not the least abashed, " so you've managed to get the mud out of Chalrey brook off you since last Tuesday. I quite thought you'd broken your neck. Do you know why you came down ? Because you didn't let your horse (who is a beauty) have the brook where *he* wanted, but pulled him about to make him have it where *you* wanted. That ducking quite served you right. It wasn't *his* fault, but *yours.*"

" I think you're right," Huson answered, laughing. " But I generally try to make my belongings do what I wish—generally contrive to do it, in fact."

He said it almost proudly, speaking only the truth, and recalling humble days, not so very long ago, in a dark clerk's office near Portsmouth Street, Lincoln's Inn Fields; recalling how dogged determination had transformed that humble clerkship, and that dark office, into the airy first-floor off Piccadilly and the luxurious little house down St George's Square way — a man whose metaphorical shoulders were as broad and pushing as his physical ones, and who knew the value of them, and had used them to such good advantage that he had come to believe there was no obstacle on the great highway that they couldn't shove out of it, if he only set them to it, and meant it.

May looked at him and laughed.

"I daresay you're a terrible person!" she said gaily. "Very persistent, I know. How you *would* speak to me. Why, I think you began last season, after you caught my hat when it blew off. Do you recollect that? I was *so* surprised as to see you get off to pick it up! And I'll tell you something that surprised me more."

"Well? I'm very anxious to hear."

"And that was to see you could get on to that tallest horse—it *was* the tallest horse that day—without a gate or a mounting block. You didn't *look* it, you know."

"Really, May, don't be so fearfully rude!" Mrs Bethray exclaimed, horrified.

But Huson laughed. It was something quite new to him to be chaffed. His life had lain, hitherto, over the Macadam of existence; it was a refreshing change to find himself on the daisy-sprinkled turf that borders it—or *should* border it—in a society bounded by woman's influence.

"I'm not joking, mother. It's quite true, every word. I *was* surprised. Hark! I'm sure that's Mrs Marfleet's cough, and Sarah's creaking boots in the hall!" and May ran out to meet the guests.

It wouldn't have been a particularly cheery dinner if it hadn't been for May, who was the life and soul of it.

Even Mrs Marfleet was obliged to laugh now and then, when the contagion became irresistible, in spite of the solemn fact that the Rev. Modred was reported to be suffering from an attack of influenza, and, in consequence, nasal to a degree approaching intelligibility

"Yes, dearest Mrs Bethray, obliged to engage help for the duty to-morrow—quite a young man too. Unfortunately, he has a squint, and a very slight impediment ; but Modred thought he would do. Will you be at church ? "

Charming Mrs Bethray feared a threatening cold might prevent ; but May would go, certainly.

May made a face.

Left alone over his wine, John Huson's face changed once or twice, as he sat turned towards the blazing fire, with a napkin on his knees. He only took one glass of port, being abstemious in all things, as becomes a man shouldering his way upwards. But he looked once or twice round the cosily furnished room, and saw a great deal more in the fittings than most people would have seen, for he saw a little golden vision everywhere. On some few points even financial agents are human.

And there was a peculiarity about that vision face that haunted him. In one way it was unlike the original, for the original varied in expression with every thought that flashed through the active brain ; but the fancy face always wore one expression, always told one tale : " I think you old enough to be my father ;

I haven't the least idea you care for me.   If
you told me so, I should laugh at you.   Still,
if you pursue me with your bull-dog per-
sistency, I shall yield to your wishes at last,
as everything else in life *has* yielded to you.
But I promise you a terrible uphill fight
first!"

On the whole satisfied with what the fancy
face told him, John Huson drank off his glass
of port, and went into the drawing-room.

Throughout the remainder of the evening,
charming Mrs Bethray managed to keep Mrs
Marfleet and Sarah close to her, so that poor
little May was obliged to talk to John Huson.
And she did it, not with a very good grace,
but still did it; and there was nothing in her
looks or words to make John Huson think that
fancy face told him a lie.   He was quite satisfied with the appearance of affairs.   He went
at his work in hand in his own way, and a
very direct way (according to his lights) it
was.

"You're very fond of horses, I suppose, Miss
Bethray?"

"I suppose I am—aren't you?"

"Yes. You never come to London, do you?"

"Smoky old London! No; I hate it."

"You like my chestnut horse so much, I wonder what you'd say to the one I drive in the phaeton? Coal black — wonderfully high action—capital mouth. Quite a pleasure to drive, I assure you."

He has found her one vulnerable point, as he finds most people's vulnerable points, sooner or later—usually sooner.

"Oh, how jolly! I should like to see him immensely!"

"If I had thought of that, I would have driven him down. Rather an expensive horse. I gave three hundred for him last year. But then he's perfect, and you have to pay for perfection, Miss Bethray."

"Black Diamond only cost a hundred—fancy three! He *must* be perfect!"

"I tell you he is. If Mrs Bethray ever asks me down again, I'll drive it, and the next day you shall drive him."

"I should enjoy it; wouldn't it be *great!*" May exclaimed enthusiastically. "What's his name?"

"I'm afraid I don't pet my horses very much. I don't use their names often; but they call him 'Satan' at the stables."

Mrs Marfleet, chancing to catch the objectionable word, in a pause of Mrs Bethray's conversation, thought it was time to be going that moment, and rose accordingly. So ended the evening.

"May, darling," her charming mother said, calling her into her own room for a moment before going to bed: "May, darling, you *are* a lucky girl!"

"Why, mother, dear?"

"Why, child? When you've evidently made an impression on Mr Huson. Equal to a Rothschild or a Baring! Glorious, May, glorious!"

And May, becoming suddenly crimson, cries out, as though in pain,—

"Oh, mother, *don't* talk such nonsense! He's old enough to be my father, and ugly enough to be—I really don't know what!" and rushes off to lay a face that contrasts strongly with it against her lace-bordered pillow.

CHAPTER THE EIGHTH.

In spite of the temptations held out to her in the shape of the squinting curate with the slight impediment in his speech, charming Mrs Bethray denied herself the pleasure of attending church that Sunday morning. Charming Mrs Bethray believed in some sort of self-denial, and she denied herself that service. But May went, and with her John Huson. It was the first time he had been in a church since childhood, and it brought back all sorts of strange recollections to him. Somehow the swelling notes of an organ always carry our hearts back to the past, and never forward to the future. There is always more of the cradle than the grave in Church music. The great charm of the whole Church Service is, that it never alters. The familiar rhythmic prayers we heard in our childish days, still echo in the ears that are dulled with age. Let everything else "move with the times" but that quaint old service, whose charm lies in its antiquity. The quaint old service we reverence, because it is the one thing remaining stationary in a world of change. There were tempered aspirations in John Huson's heart as he sat with May in the Grange pew that Sunday morning—aspirations not towards gold, but virtue—a longing that the record of the past was purer, clearer, and some dark spots in it vanished away. For the time, and the time only, John Huson had nothing of the bull-dog about him, and he looked with something almost like pity in his eyes at the fair young girl, in the glory of her innocence, whom her mother was selling to satisfy the basest ends.

The sleepy congregation, the earthy air, the singing that was not wholly in tune; the rays of changing sunlight that penetrated the building in shafts, and flecked the walls with re-flected colours from the stained-glass windows

May, singing sweetly, with an especial ray of her own upon her—a ray that made a sunny glory round her golden hair; all these things combined to make John Huson feel, as he had not felt for years. If there were anything that marred and hardened the soft effect of that church that day, it lay in the stern, unbending righteousness of Mrs Marfleet's face, and the dogmatic declamation of the young curate with the squint and the impediment.

All the other lights and shadows fluttering in the church changed their positions as the service advanced; but the golden glory of May's especial ray lingered, as though loth to leave so fair a hovering place, and was on her to the last, as she knelt a moment after the benediction. John Huson noticed it as he passed his coat sleeve round his hat, and waited for her to raise her head.

"What are London churches like—their services, I mean?" she asked as they walked back towards the Grange together.

For the life of him, looking in those bright,

honest eyes, he couldn't tell her he never went to London churches.

"Very dark and dreary," he said, hazarding a guess.

"Ah, I should think so," she answered innocently. "Did you see our angels, those carved ones in the chancel? I always envy those wings. Fancy flying through space and not being tired! Of course, angels are never tired like mortals are. It must be delightful to be an angel!"

She didn't look very far removed from one, with the sunshine on her golden hair, and John Huson told her so.

"Is that meant for a compliment?" she asked, looking at him surprised, and *so* surprised that for a moment (the bull-dog having hardly returned in full vigour then) he felt sorry for his remark, felt almost ashamed of it. But he told himself (the-bull dog coming back stronger every moment) such feelings were absurd, and said gaily,—

"No compliment at all—the plain truth."

She looked at him a moment, and then laughed.

"I don't feel anything of the wings," she said.

Charming Mrs Bethray was at the drawing-room window, watching for them as they came up the avenue.

"You looked *so* jolly together, you can't think!" she exclaimed effusively to May, who entered the room whilst Huson was hanging up his hat and taking off his gloves in the hall. "How do you like him, dear?"

"He's not so bad *for a middle-aged man,* you know," May answered, laughing. "But his best point is his horses. He tells me he has a black that must be a beauty, mother. I am *so* anxious to see it! He says he will drive it down here the next time you ask him to come. I *do* want to see that horse! Couldn't you ask him soon, mother?"

Charming Mrs Bethray laughed softly to herself, looked at the little golden vision she was luring into a trap, without the least compunction in her face, and answered,—

"I don't see why we shouldn't ask him here *next* Saturday, dear, if *you* wish it. You had better ask him, I think—it will come better from you. But, I tell you, it is rather marked, May"

"Oh, who's to mark it, mother? It's not the man, but the horse, I want. Nobody could think I wanted the *man.*"

Charming Mrs Bethray laughed again, her schemes were working so satisfactorily.

John Huson came in presently, and May, all laughing innocence, preferred her request.

"Then you could drive down with Satan, couldn't you?" she asked eagerly. "It would be so jolly."

"I will drive down with pleasure," John Huson said.

Mrs Bethray expressed herself delighted, and so the thing was settled, and they all went in to luncheon gaily.

It was only that afternoon, when May took the guest to see some ruins in the neighbourhood, at charming Mrs Bethray's special suggestion, that May noticed a change in John Huson's manner—a change that rather frightened her, and made her repent her recent invitation. An indistinct feeling was with her that afternoon that some influence was upon her which she could not combat. A feeling that she had got into the full current of fate, and was being carried very rapidly out to sea. Of the action of a strong will upon a weaker, she knew nothing at all, or she would have understood what that feeling was.

"Only to think of the absurdity of such a thing!" she told herself, alone in her own room, afterwards. "He certainly squeezed my hand, getting over that last stile, and did it on purpose, I'm certain; and I was *so* angry. I should have said something—but, somehow, I couldn't—especially when I thought of the black horse. I *must* drive that black horse! And it will tease Charley so—or it would tease him if he were at home to see. Poor old Charley! I wonder how he is getting on with that old crossed-in-love uncle? I wonder when he'll write and tell me the day of his return?"

Her conscience told her she had been rather neglecting poor old Charley in her thoughts, and it was this sudden remembrance of him that made her hastily replace the hat she had just taken off, and steal downstairs and out of the house, to make the fairest picture of the day in the silver mirror at Hollybush stile.

Finding no one there to speak to, she was obliged to improvise a fancy listener from one of the holly bushes.

"Poor old Charley! There is nobody else half so jolly in the world—though you *are* a Poet:—and I am dreadfully miserable without you."

So she told the holly bush.

"Well, then, we hope to see you on Saturday next?" charming Mrs Bethray asked her guest the last thing as they parted that night.

John Huson looked at May, and said,—

"The answer rests with Miss Bethray—am I to come?"

And May thought of the perfect black horse, and answered in all simplicity,—

"Oh, yes, do—driving, of course."

That night Mrs Bethray hugged her daughter most affectionately.

"Oh, May, May! you *are* a lucky girl!" she exclaimed enthusiastically, and only laughed immoderately when May pressed her for the reason.

CHAPTER THE NINTH.

A MONTH later, and, at the usual hour, Charles Darrac stood beside the silver mirror and the falling brook, leaning over the stile looking for May's coming.

The days were lengthening, and a rustling breeze stirred through the leafless branches, as though Nature were awakening with a sigh. On the topmost bough of a beech tree near, a thrush whistled clear to a great crimson sunset.

The breeze rustled through the wood once more, the brook plashed softly into the silver mirror down below, and May Bethray came round the bend, and met her lover face to face.

He held out his arms, and would have

embraced her after his long absence, but she stopped him.

"No," she said, "you mustn't; not on any account, till you've heard everything—*everything*, Charley. And it's all so strange, I don't know how to begin, or how to go on when I have begun—I really don't."

Charley Darrac, looking at her in surprise, saw a new May Bethray standing there before him. Quite a different May to the childish, laughing, happy one he had parted with at that stile only a month ago — different with an indescribable difference, that pained the man looking at it unspeakably

"Let me see if I can help you," he says, tenderly taking one of the little hands that rest upon the stile near him. "Well, as you will," for she takes the hand away with a rapid gesture; "only let us see where we are. A month ago I was called away on what I thought only a short absence, and you specially forbade me to write to you till I could name the date of my return. I was to write then, and then only. That time proved a long time, as my uncle wished me to remain with him in the capacity of private secretary till he could find another to replace his late one, who is dead. I consent, still, according to our agreement, unable to write and explain the longer absence. Before I am in a position to write, I receive a letter from you—a very hurried and perplexing letter—in which you say that you don't know how it is, but that you seem to be engaged, and ask me to come off here at once. I plead the most unheard-of reasons for a short return here, to my uncle, and get a day. Here I am in consequence, utterly dazed and confused as to what it all means. Please explain what has been happening, and whether you are joking, or in terrible earnest."

"Terrible earnest, Charley; there never *was* any one more in terrible earnest than I am. It's fearful, and *so* confusing. But, somehow, it happened like this: Mr Huson, as you know, was coming down before you left. Well, he came down, and was very civil to me, and mother said I had 'made an impression'—those were her words. During that visit he mentioned a wonderful black horse he drove in his phaeton in London. You know I'm mad about horses. I wanted to see it. He said he would drive it down, and did so, the next Saturday. It *was* such a beauty! Oh, Charley, you don't know what a beauty that horse is! I drove it, and was in love with it. I told Mr Huson so; and the phaeton was awfully jolly too, red and black, with an 'H' on the panels. Well, on the Monday, Mr Huson, who had been very pleasant to me, was to go to town by train, and his man was to take the horse up the following day. Mr Huson *did* go up to town by train. That very evening came a letter from him for me, begging me to accept the horse and phaeton, and asking me to look inside the driving-box. I *was so* delighted I didn't know what to do, Charley. He is so rich, you know, the present was nothing to him—rich, mother says, as a Rothschild or Baring. Of course, I looked in the driving-box, and there I found, oh, such a splendid large package of chocolate, and—and— a little ring. It was *such* a beauty! I didn't think any harm, you know, as he was so old,

and so rich; and I asked mother, and she said
I was to write a civil letter, and thank him
for all the presents, which I did. And I wore
the ring, and then, the next day, horrible Mrs
Marfleet came and congratulated me upon *my
engagement*, and mother said, of course, I was
engaged; and then Mr Huson came and actually — actually wanted to kiss me, Charley—
there!"

Charley Darrac's face had been growing graver
as the story was unfolded to him, and now he
says, very seriously,—

"You have been acting very sillily, Daisy.
You couldn't have acted more sillily."

"I knew you'd be angry. I was certain* of
it!" poor May says, and beginning to cry;
"and you hav'n't heard the worst of it yet."

"Why, what more is there?"

"Oh, a lot! The chocolate looked *so* awfully
jolly, I *couldn't* help eating it, you know" (sobbing), "and—and Mr Huson sent a man—who—
painted out the 'H' on the panels of the phaeton
—yes, he did—and only painted it out *very thin*
—and didn't put 'B' there; and I'm sure the

painting out will all wash off—and you can see what *that* means, and what his idea is, can't you ? *I* can."

In spite of his anger and annoyance, Charles Darrac can hardly help laughing, and she sees it.

" I don't think there's anything to laugh at in it !" she says bitterly. " Everybody thinks we're engaged—and Mr Huson does, too—and he always rides close to me out hunting, and is always coming here — and — and — I know I shall be married to him one of these days without knowing it — and I don't suppose you'll mind *that* the very least little bit ? "

" Don't be silly, Daisy. Let us think what's the best to be done."

" Well—what *is* best to be done ?—that's why I wrote to you—to see if you could think what that is."

" I confess I don't see, at the moment, you've muddled the whole thing so. What did you say when Mrs Marfleet congratulated you ? Didn't you deny it ? "

" Well, you see, I had accepted the horse and phaeton — *such* a horse, Charley ! — and mother was so strong on the point; said I *couldn't* deny it, in face of the horse and phaeton — that — that — I didn't say anything."

"That was fearfully silly ! It was tacitly giving your consent. Don't you see that ? "

" But I didn't *then*, Charley. It was all so gradual; and mother being on Mr Huson's side so, you've no idea how gradual it was, Charley. If it had been a conspiracy, it couldn't have been more delicately managed—it really couldn't. What *am* I to do ? "

She looks up at him with the tears in her eyes. Those eyes that only knew smiles a month ago, and he answers her,—

" I really hardly know, Daisy. You had better see your mother to-night, and have it out with her. Have it out *bravely*, you know. Stick to your point."

" And see you here to-morrow evening ? "

" Most unfortunately, I *must* go back to my uncle to-morrow. I *can't* help it. He made that a condition of sparing me yester-day."

May begins to cry again.

"You'll find me married to Mr Huson when you return, I know you will!" she says, sobbing. "They seem to make things *fit in so*. And I'm a little afraid of Mr Huson. When he looks at me, I'm obliged to do what he wishes. It's awful, Charley, to be left to him and mother when you're away."

"You must do as I say, and have it out with Mrs Bethray to-night. That's the only way. She won't force the man upon you if you don't wish, I'm certain. It's not quite so serious a matter as you fancy, Daisy, after all."

"Ah, but it is, Charley Don't you see? I've worn the ring, and eaten the chocolate, and driven the horse and phaeton. It's fear-fully serious!"

He was obliged to laugh again, he couldn't help it. Her earnestness was so real, and she evidently thought herself so utterly helpless in the matter.

" You're heartless because you're a Poet. That's it!" she says, looking up at him through her tears. "All Poets are! They've a beautiful ear, but they've no heart—they're all alike—every one!"

"Don't be silly, Daisy." Charley Darrac says. "Now I've heard it all, I may take your hand —you know there's nobody in the world I love as I love you."

"Yes, there is. I daresay, there's a whole host of people you love better than me," May says defiantly, not quite decided to leave off crying.

" What nonsense! Who, for instance?"

"Oh, how can *I* tell? Heaps—your old crossed-in-love uncle—I've no doubt; and, very likely, some awful old fright or other besides. Sarah Marfleet, perhaps."

"Now, you're jealous, Daisy."

"Do you think I'm jealous of *you?* You—*a Poet?* I only wrote because I thought you could set it all right, and you can't; of course, you can't. I might have known that! And what's the use of being a Poet, if you can't help a girl out of an engagement she has got into without knowing, just through—"

"Wearing a ring, and eating chocolate, and driving a horse and phæton, eh, Daisy?"

"You *won't* see how serious it is! You positively *won't!*" poor May exclaims in great distress. "All you can do is to joke, or *try* to joke — you're not clever enough to joke *really* — and — and — go away again. I'm sorry I wrote. I'm sorry I didn't settle it myself in a way I've thought of—a way I *will* settle it in too!" (with sudden determination).

"What way is that, Daisy?"

"I sha'n't tell you anything more about it! Go back to you old crossed-in-love uncle! He's the best society for—a Poet! Yes, he is! Good-bye. I'm going!"

Charles Darrac gets lightly over the stile before she is aware, and slips a detaining arm round her.

"Now, don't be silly, Daisy," he says firmly, "We're not going to part like this, I tell you plainly."

"Yes, we are!"

" No, we're not—look up at me."

" No, I won't ! "

" Come, come, Daisy, do be rational. I can't help going away to-morrow — let us part friends."

How long are we going to part for this time —a year or so ? " she asks, looking down, but relenting a little.

" Nonsense—a month or so, at the outside limit."

" I know you'll find me married—or—or something else horrid—when you return."

" But you'll write to me, won't you ? *Do* write, Daisy. I shall expect you to."

" I don't know that I shall. It all depends. I shall see."

" This is not a very satisfactory understanding, Daisy."

" It isn't an understanding at all—I don't understand anything. I'm muddled."

" Well, do you understand that you are to have it out seriously with Mrs Bethray to-night ? "

" Yes, I understand that ; and I also under-

stand that I must be going home now—
there's the dressing-bell!" (trying to disengage
herself).

"And do you understand this further fact"
(stooping very close to her ear, and whispering), "that I'm miserable at leaving you, and
wouldn't do it on any account, only that our
future comfort depends upon my being on
good terms with my uncle? Do you understand *that*, darling?"

She looks up at him for one lightning
moment, tells him that she does understand it,
proves it by throwing her arms round his neck
and hugging him, and then, getting free, is out
of sight, round the bend of the pathway, in an
instant.

Charles Darrac goes to the bend, and calls
after her, laughing: "Say good-bye, Daisy!"
She pauses a moment, turning a glowing face
—something of the old happy face—back to
him, says "Good-bye—Poet!" and blows him
another kiss, laughing too.

So they part, those two, and pausing a moment
at the stile to light a cigar, Darrac looks at the

silver mirror and the falling brook, and wonders idly how they will look the next time he stands there.

How *will* they look next time?

Never again, to Charles Darrac, as they looked that night!

CHAPTER THE TENTH.

CHARMING Mrs Bethray was especially sweet to her daughter during dinner that night. Charming Mrs Bethray had indeed been especially sweet to her daughter ever since that first visit of John Huson. But on the night that was to see May speak plainly to her mother, charming Mrs Bethray was in a happier frame of mind than usual, reason being a letter, come by the evening post, from Roland Vance—letter of a particularly affectionate tone, with the sweetest allusions in it to the old letters of the old days, and the apple woman at the square corner who used to be Cupid's postman. Only natural that in such a communication—coming straight from Roland Vance's heart—there should be embodied the faintest breath of a subject very near that heart, and of a material nature. There was so much sentiment in that letter, indeed, that the little materialism, carried in the faintest passing reference to John Huson and business, was quite refreshing. Besides, it proved dear Roland so honest and straightforward, Laura told herself.

Something in that letter made charming Mrs Bethray take especial pains with her toilet, though mother and daughter were to dine alone. Even for her, she looked a great many times in her glass before going down into the drawing-room; and each time she looked she saw more milestones there.

Very annoying! Why should vain, frivolous, stupid dolls ever fade, and become only boring? Too bad, ever so much! Shows plainly something very wrong in the universal scheme somewhere.

Charming Mrs Bethray had two gowns spread out on the bed before her—a black one, and a white—and sat lounging in a chair before her fire quite ten minutes, in a state of indecision. Which should it be?

The maid thought perhaps the black, as there was nobody dining.

Laura shut her up sharply.

"*Don't* speak at such a moment! Can't you see I'm thinking? I had nearly decided when you spoke. Go into the dressing-room, and wait there till I call. I shouldn't like to decide too hurriedly, and I *must* have quiet—absolute quiet—when I think."

Left alone, Mrs Bethray rose and took a further survey of herself in her looking-glass— a critical survey, with a candle held very close to aid her sight. The result was a sigh.

"I don't know how it is! I used to be *downy*, and now I see no down at all, anywhere. May is downy — most beautifully downy—like a peach. It's very irritating. I suppose London air, and late hours, and all that sort of thing, is bad for down on one's face. Yes; it must be that, and nothing else."

Of course it must, charming Mrs Bethray! That, or the electric telegraph, or the mania for long alpen - stock - handled parasols — anything but the little fact that you are getting older!

It was written in the book of the Costume Fates that the black gown should be worn that night, and the maid was summoned from the dressing-room presently to effect it.

Meanwhile May, with only fifteen minutes available to pit against the sixty her mother dawdled away over her dressing, came down in the airiest blue, an angel of light. Such a daughter would have gladdened most mother's hearts. Charming Mrs Bethray looked her over critically, and—sighed. Still the thought flashed through her mind that May was older in appearance; older, that is to say, by an increased graveness in her face, where the childish gaiety that used to be so noticeable was fading day by day. Even to charming Mrs Bethray's not very keen powers of observation, there was a new expression in May's face that night — an expression she could not read. It was a *firmer* face than she had ever seen before.

"May, take some of this sherry; it is just the thing for you," her mother said, when the meal was pretty well advanced.

"No, thanks, mother. Really, I don't care for any wine. I had rather not."

"Nonsense, May. Take some at once."

The child had been so obedient before, in everything, this sudden insubordination was most surprising.

Charming Mrs Bethray pressed the sherry. May remained firm.

"Really, May, I wish you to take some."

"But I had rather not, mother. You can't wish me to take it if I don't want it, surely."

"I *do* wish it, because you don't know what's good for you. You never do."

"I am sorry to differ with you, but I think I *do* know what is best; and I hate sherry, especially dry sherry. I really won't take any."

Evidently a new phase of character had come with the new face.

Quite wonderful how obstinate charming Mrs Bethray could be on occasion.

"I must insist, May—I positively must. You seem entirely to forget I have some right to obedience."

May didn't speak. There was a water-jug standing within reach, and to settle the matter more effectually, she took it and filled her sherry glass with water.

Charming Mrs Bethray, noting the action, noted something else: that John Huson's ring was not upon the little hand that held the jug. She opened her mouth to speak, saw the servant in attendance, closed her mouth again without speaking — remained silent the rest of the meal.

"May, come and sit here by me."

They were in the drawing-room, and alone at last.

May went and sat down on a hassock at her mother's feet, but the face turned to the fire was still the same firm face.

"Where is Mr Huson's ring, dear?"

"Upstairs, in its case, on my dressing-table, mother."

"Why don't you wear it?"

"Because I thought—that is, you seemed to think—it meant that I was engaged to Mr Huson."

"May, what nonsense is this? You *are* engaged to Mr Huson. *He* understands it so, and *we* understand it so. Of course, you are. An immensely lucky girl, too, to get such a husband."

May sits quiet a moment, looking down at the dancing flames, then she says,—

"Mother, that's why I wanted to have a talk with you. It's all a terrible mistake. I don't care for Mr Huson the very least little bit, I don't, indeed. I couldn't think of marrying him, I couldn't, really. It would be *too* dreadful. You've misunderstood me, mother, all along."

This was fearful, after the prosperous way the scheme proceeded at first. Charming Mrs Bethray grasped the arms of her chair, and glared at her daughter quite fiercely.

"Don't talk such rubbish, May I won't hear it! You ought to be thankful to me for having provided you with such a man. It is horribly ungrateful to behave like this. I wouldn't have believed it of you. It would be outrageous conduct on your part to throw him over *now*, after accepting his presents — *such* presents, too. You *can't* do it! You *sha'n't* do it!"

Not if charming Mrs Bethray could help it, she shouldn't. Not while Roland Vance's allegiance depended directly upon it. What was May's happiness scaled against that of charming Mrs Bethray's own?

"But it isn't a *real* engagement, it isn't, really, mother. He never actually asked me, in so many words, to have him. If he had, I should have said no at once. It's so unsatisfactory. I seem to have *drifted* into it, without being consulted."

In spite of her courage, tears began to glitter in May's eyes.

"You *will* be asked on Saturday, I'm certain —positive of it—and you will say 'Yes.' I am sure you will, for my sake."

"What is it to *you*, mother? I am so young— not eighteen yet, think of that. You *can't* want me to marry when I don't want too. I don't understand it all—I don't a bit."

"There is no need for you to understand it.

At your age, girls do what they're told to do. You'll understand it all, by-and-by."

"I'm sure I sha'n't, mother. I *won't* be hurried into it like this, either. I'm quite determined. I won't."

"You're a heartless, ungrateful child, and you make me cry," Mrs Bethray says, and does cry a little, she is so vexed at the prospect of losing Roland Vance.

"I'm sorry to make you cry, mother; but really, I *can't* accept him — I can't, indeed," May replies, not a long way from crying either.

A beautifully preserved specimen of the mercenary mother charming Mrs Bethray made, sitting there in a graceful attitude, endeavouring, by force or persuasion, to sacrifice her daughter to the god gold—or to a worse. Huson's train of thought, the first time he saw her, was quite right; she would have made an excellent Brahmin priestess.

"You have placed me in a terrible position, May. You have thoroughly deceived me. Only think a moment. By accepting those presents,

I thought at once you liked him. Why, don't you recollect asking him yourself to come down again the first time he was in the house? Don't you recollect him standing in this very room, when I asked him if he *were* coming, and his turning to you, and saying, 'The answer rests with Miss Bethray—shall I come, Miss Bethray?' and you said 'Yes' to that marked question. Don't you remember all that?"

"Yes; but—I had no idea—not the faintest—"

"That is all nonsense, May. You're not a fool; no one can call you that. Besides, I had cautioned you, positively cautioned you. I said: 'If we have him down again next Saturday, it will look very *marked*, May,' and you only laughed. What *could* I think? And then the beautiful presents. And when Mrs Marfleet congratulated you on the engagement, (which she oughtn't to have done, in strict etiquette; she should have congratulated Mr Huson *then*, and *you* on your *marriage*), why, even then, you only looked foolish, and said nothing. It's amazing, May! What *could* I think? When, last

week, Mr Huson asked me whether you were
happy in your engagement, of course I said
'Yes;' and he said he would speak to you
plainly about it next time he came down, which
will be Saturday, you know See what a position you have put me in if you go and upset
everything then—only think!"

It sounded all wonderfully honest and sincere,
as charming Mrs Bethray spoke it, with great
earnestness and rapidity.

Still May's firm face looked straight into the
fire.

"I can't help it, mother; I really can't. I
should have no further pleasure in life if I had
to marry Mr Huson. Even as it is, people are
wondering why I haven't been out with the
hounds so often as usual; *that's* the reason,
of course. I can't bear to be so much with
him. I won't hunt at all if this nonsense goes
on."

"Nonsense, May! Nonsense! You call the
chance of marrying a man equal to a Rothschild
or a Baring nonsense! Fancy what he could
give you! The gowns, the diamonds, the car-

riages! There wouldn't be a woman in London better turned out than you would be—only imagine it!"

"But I like the country best, ever so much the best, you forget that, mother."

"What is your life in the country, May? Recall it: a ride through the lanes, or a gallop with hounds; a drive somewhere or other to make a call in the afternoon; a lonely run through the damp shrubberies before dinner— what's there to like in *that* life, day after day?"

"Everything I care for," May answered truly, her eyes dim with visions of Hollybush stile and its present loneliness.

"It's no good talking to such a girl," her mother said bitterly. "But, all the same, you'll have to bend, May. I tell you distinctly, you will."

"Why, mother? Why, if I don't want to?" asked poor May, terribly distressed, and finding herself, for the first time, in conflict with a mother who had hitherto taken no interest in her existence.

"Why, if she didn't want to ?" Charming Mrs Bethray covered her face with four square inches of cambric and lace border, and threw herself back in her chair, apparently plunged in deeper grief, but in reality taking time to consider whether she should play her highest card then, or reserve it for a more desperate occasion later on. Finally, she decides upon the later course, and says in an injured tone,—

"Because it's for your interest that you should encourage John Huson, dear; that you should marry John Huson, May Remember that—to your interest. It is so much to your interest that you should marry him, that I couldn't go on caring for a child so utterly foolish, so utterly blind to her own advantage. I really think we shall be obliged to part, May."

May started up in surprise, but quite firm still.

"I can't help it; if we have to part, mother. I can't marry him."

Charming Mrs Bethray pretended to cry a little. It was no use: the same resolute face looked at the fire, the same resolute voice answered her,—

"I *can't* marry him."

All charming Mrs Bethray could do was to ask her to "think again."

"But I *have* thought, mother, over and over again, and I am as firm as ever. I can't understand your sudden anxiety. I really can't. Why, you know, you've hardly taken any notice of me before this, and now—no!—it's impossible. I *can't* marry him! It seems to me it is so entirely a matter for myself, and no one else. If any one else were concerned— you, for instance—it would be different; but as it is—no, I can't, mother. There!" and May got up from her footstool, and went over to the piano.

Again charming Mrs Bethray put her cambric before her face, and wondered whether she should play her highest card then or later. May's words had led up to it. But, no! That must be a very last resource, when every other had been tried and failed.

She rose presently and went across to May

playing valses at the piano. Laying her hands upon the pretty shoulders, she stooped down and kissed her.

"At anyrate. we are friends, May? At anyrate, you think I have tried to do what was best for you?"

May's warm heart went out to her in a moment. She turned upon the music-stool, and threw her arms about her mother's neck.

"I'm sure of it; certain and positive, mother" (kissing her the while); "and I'm *so* sorry I can't do my part of the arrangement. But I don't care for him—not the least, you know, and *you* wouldn't have married a man you didn't love, would you, mother?"

How was May to know her mother had married Mr Bethray, not caring for him in the least, from prudential reasons, with a heart wholly gone to penniless Roland Vance? She knew nothing whatever of this; didn't even notice that charming Mrs Bethray failed to answer the question, but said,—

"One thing I want you to promise me, May—about Saturday. You will think the

matter over carefully between this and then
—very carefully. If by Friday night you
can't make a favourable answer to him the
next day, tell me. I must know it beforehand.
I really must. It is terribly important I should
know. It is all so much more serious than
you believe, May. Perhaps (if after seeing me
on Friday night you are still firm) I could
then break it to him myself, and so save you
the pain of refusing him."

In the depth of her gratitude May hugged
her mother again and again, and told her how
good she was, and that no other girl ever had
such a sweet, darling one before. All which
endearments charming Mrs Bethray took very
philosophically, and assured her daughter she
had only her child's interest at heart.

And nothing happened. The drawing-room
floor remained unopened. Charming Mrs Bethray
unswallowed up. Justice has gone to sleep in
these times: or at anyrate, has ceased to act in
the direct manner it used to do according to
ancient histories. Your righteous may prosper ;
but your unrighteous are sure to. A noble, far-

I

reaching, intellectual age this of ours, in which we scoff at all faiths and all idols, and yet in secret have our own faith, and our own idol. We have set Humbug up on high, and worship him, day and night. He is our religion: a more easy and practical one than any other, claiming more devout, unwavering followers than all the rest put together.

Charming Mrs Bethray dropped into a peaceful sleep that night, conscious that the game was in her hands in spite of May's seeming obstinacy "I have touched her *heart*," she told herself, and dozed off satisfied forthwith, to dream happy dreams of Roland Vance.

CHAPTER THE ELEVENTH.

THOUGH she had been firm and resolute, May felt very unhappy after that interview with her mother. Somehow the tide seemed bearing her more and more swiftly to the ocean. Her mother, in some mysterious way, had conveyed the impression that something more lay behind; an awful intangible something, liable to take visible shape at any moment. Whilst charming Mrs Bethray dreamed happy dreams of Roland Vance, the innocent child, who was to be sacrified for him, lay sleepless and fearful, listening to the rustling breeze, and watching the twinkling stars.

Poor little isolated May, trying to read her fate, and failing woefully!

A misty morning found her walking rapidly among the shrubberies, disconsolate.

Charming Mrs Bethray had not appeared at breakfast, and May had taken that meal alone, and gone out to get close to Nature, and borrow peace of mind from her if she could.

The laurels in the shrubberies dripped tears upon the sodden earth, the boughs of the great leafless trees shed floods of tears as the wind swept through them: A sad grey day, without a smile of sunshine anywhere.

Round and about the shrubbery walks May went, walking quickly, deep in thought, seeing nothing of things about her till she came upon the silver mirror and the falling brook, and then everything became visible to her with a suddenness that was like a blow. As she stood there, leaning over the stile and looking down, the silver mirror never reflected so sad a face before.

While she stood there, thinking of a hundred happy meetings, wondering when the next would be—whether it would *ever* be—a quick footstep of some one invisible round the bend of the path, startled her, and she raised a glowing face suddenly, with a wild, momentary hope making her heart beat fast.

She conquered the idea the next moment: "How absurd!" she told herself, "as if a poet would wear creaking boots! It's Sarah Marfleet! Of course it is!"

And it was Sarah Marfleet, looking rather more equine and righteous than usual. Looking fully twenty-blank; but especially the blank.

"Dear me, May! Who would have thought of seeing you here!" she exclaimed, getting over the stile with amazing awkwardness, and shaking hands.

"Why not? I'm taking exercise, that's all. Come and have a turn or two with me—will you?"

"Well, I was going to call on Mrs Bethray as to her subscription to the coal club, which she has forgotten to pay this year. I'm in no particular hurry though. What a very awkward stile that is! I've never (but once, I think) come this way before. Shall we go in this direction?"

They went accordingly, side by side; May, and the only woman friend she had.

"You are very silent, May!" Sarah Marfleet said presently, when they had made one or two circles of the shrubbery without exchanging a word.

"Yes, Sarah. I'm not very well—that is, not very cheerful. In fact, I'm worried."

"Has Black Diamond—or the new horse—gone lame?"

"Oh, no! Black Diamond—is never lame, nor anything she ought not to be; and the other horse—that's all right enough. But Sarah, that other horse is connected with my trouble, almost the sole cause of it. I wonder what you would say if I told you all about it?"

"I'm afraid I'm no authority upon horses," Sarah replies. Nobody ever knew her take a meaning unless it was beaten into her by the heaviest of sledge-hammer words. This is a distinct feature of superlative righteousness.

May sighed. It *was* hard to have only such a confidant and adviser.

"Oh! it's nothing to do with horses, Sarah!

Nothing directly to do with them, at least. It's about Mr Huson, Sarah—and about—heart and—and feelings, you know."

Sarah Marfleet said "Oh!" in a tone conveying that she might be of some use there, though, judging from her equine style of face, she should have been far more useful on the other subject.

"This is my difficulty," May said, unconsciously walking on faster in her excitement as she spoke. "This is my difficulty: I'm supposed to be engaged to Mr Huson."

"Supposed, May? Why, we all think you *are* engaged to him, and Mrs Bethray has said as much."

"That's just it, I'm not *really* engaged to him, you know. I've *drifted* into it. That's the word, Sarah, *drifted*. He has never asked me in so many words to marry him. I couldn't refuse him, you see, in consequence. It's most unsatisfactory, Sarah, and that's what's bothering me so much."

Sarah (whose practical experience in love-affairs was confined to a rushlight passion experienced ten years ago for a deacon—a passion promptly extinguished by Mrs Marfleet's wisdom) considered a moment, and then said with her habitual inaccuracy of aim,—

"No doubt, though, he *will* propose some day."

"Oh, Sarah! Can't you see it's not that! I don't want him to. I don't really care the tiniest bit for him. Mother is forcing me into it, Sarah. Forcing me by every means in her power. Oh, Sarah! you're the only friend I have; think a moment, and tell me that I *can't* marry a man I don't care for! Tell me, even though mother *does* wish it, that it would be wrong to deceive Mr Huson! Tell me this. *Do* Sarah!" Poor little May turned a troubled face to Sarah Marfleet's equine one, making the strongest appeal for the support she felt so necessary in the coming trials. She might as well have appealed to Cleopatra's Needle on the Thames Embankment!

"Oh! Mrs Bethray thinks you ought to marry Mr Huson, does she?" Miss Marfleet asked.

" Yes. She wishes it very much—presses it very much; but, Sarah, what *has* my mother to do with it ? Is it not solely my affair, and mine only ? "

" ' Your own feelings should be under control, May,' that is my reply. In all cases of doubt like this there is a law far above personal inclinations. *That* is the law by which to guide your course. You ask me ? I have only one answer, and not *my* answer, but a higher : ' Children obey your parents,' nothing can be placed above *that*. So that we must bend, like supple rods, May."

Miss Marfleet looked like anything but a supple rod herself, and utterly incapable of bending, as she paced along beside golden May, rigidly upright. Perhaps something of this struck her, however, even in the depths of her sorrow, for she said quietly,—

" But we *can't* always bend, Sarah ! We may break right short off—we *may*, you know."

" Then we *must* break right short off—no matter *how* short. There is but one law, we have to take that as it stands—as it is written.

Not looking to this side of it, or to that side of it, but straight at it, the letter of it. I know there are vain mortals going about talking of the Spirit of the Law. They are deceived, May—hopelessly deceived! I take it as it is written—wholly—in its entirety. It applies to every case—to yours as to another's: 'Children obey your parents.' There is nothing said about inclinations, or hopes, or dislikings. It is plain, very plain. By it you must abide."

There was such an intensity in the words—such a delight in crushing out some spark of "will," some base inclination—such an upholding of the letter that killeth, and debasing of the spirit that giveth life—that Sarah Marfleet placed herself upon a very high pedestal in the great gallery of saints forthwith.

"Oh, Sarah, Sarah! is there *no* hope?" May pleaded, almost in tears.

"None but in bending."

"But I know I shall break—short off—*very* short off.

"If so, such is your destiny, that is all—a sad destiny; but most destinies *are* sad. Better to be broken short off by obeying the law, than utterly annihilàted by *dis*-obeying it."

It wasn't so very clear to May that this was so; but she didn't say anything. She began to cry.

Sarah seemed quite cheered up at the sight of the tears. They were, she said, a sign of humility and bending. She left May to them, and went indoors gaily after the coal club money, leaving May pacing round and round the shrubberies alone.

"They are all against me, but I know I'm right," she told herself through her tears, making another sad picture in the silver mirror.

But she didn't stay there long. She couldn't remain there in her isolation. The place was haunted by visions of Charles Darrac. Dear Charley! How lonely she was without him! She walked quickly away and indoors, by a deft manœuvre avoiding the drawing-room window and Sarah Marflect. She went through the loungy old hall, straight to the library, where the fumes of John Huson's last week's cigar still hung in the air, and sitting down at a writing-table took up a pen and began to think, nibbling the end of the pen the while to stimulate her meditation. Yes; it seemed almost as though she were going to talk to him, and the pen soon began to speed over the paper. Oh, the pen, the pen! sweet companion of our brightest and our darkest hours! What burning thoughts, what agonised hearts, have been shrieked away with the shrieking of a quill! The grey goose cackles on the common—a year or two—and that grey goose's plume in the master's hand, is carving immortal inscriptions on the monuments of Time! Not surprising geese should strut sometimes—Stratford geese especially—through whose ancestors' plumage came the Bard's undying words! Geese have almost a prescriptive right to strut—would have an indisputable one, if (in some hands) their plumes did not cackle far louder than ever their rightful owners used to do.

May, having written her letter, read it over fondly once or twice, as going straight to *him* to be *his* property for ever:—

"MY DEAR POET,—I am terribly afraid of writing to you, knowing you're so awfully particular (as a poet) about punctuation—which I never *could* understand, and spelling — of which I'm often doubtful. I had it out with mother last night, and was *very firm.* I think she understood me. But, Charley, there is something more behind it all than I understand. I am sure there is! I wish I knew what it is. I've been to-day to the stile, and it *does* look so cold and so lonely, you can't think *how* cold and lonely! I suppose you won't be coming home for *years and years?* I don't know, but I think I'll send back the horse and pha— you know—the carriage Mr Huson gave me with the horse. I'm not sure how you spell it. I think I'll send them both back. He is coming on Saturday, and then I'm going to refuse him utterly. That is only the day after to-morrow, as to-day is Thursday. I haven't been hunting, and people are talking about it; but I don't like being with him so much. You understand, don't you? The last meet of the season is on Tuesday next. I sha'n't go—unless I clearly make him see it's all over—in which case I might. That is the luncheon-bell (I don't want any—not a bit). Good-bye, Charley. How is old crossed-in-love? I think perhaps you might answer this.

"I am very much inclined to write,—Yours always, DAISY.

"*P.S.*—But *I haven't done it, you know.*"

So she enveloped her letter, and went in to luncheon almost cheerful once more.

CHAPTER THE TWELFTH.

THE soft blue eyes of charming Mrs Bethray were often on her daughter, critically, during the time intervening between the interview in the drawing-room and the Friday night. But she never alluded to the subject; she was far too sharp for that. She merely speculated how far that last card she held would go towards winning the game she meant to win at any cost. Typical of how little she really knew of her daughter's heart, that she was utterly ignorant of May's love for Charles Darrac What May chose to do in her charming mother's absence, her charming mother had cared less than nothing about hitherto.

Sarah Marfleet had told charming Mrs Bethray (considering it, in her righteousness, a duty) the whole of May's confidence in the shrubbery as to John Huson, and charming Mrs Bethray had thanked Sarah cordially, and doubled her subscription to the coal club there and then: such information of the state of May's heart was worth something. Moreover, it told Laura plainly that the highest card her mendacity had procured her, must be played on Friday night. That Friday was the one before Easter, and it was spent by mother and daughter in assisting Mrs Marfleet and Sarah to decorate Fairacres Church for the coming festival. Charming Mrs Bethray didn't do very much herself; but she stood in graceful attitudes, and talked pleasantly, in a subdued tone out of deference to the building, and admired every effort Mrs Marfleet produced by ivy leaves and wreaths; indeed, she walked all the way back to the Grange, and, under her own supervision, the greenhouse was denuded of its best flowering plants, which she had conveyed to the church in a wheelbarrow with some matting over them. No wonder that, to Mrs Marfleet and Sarah, she was ten times more charming than ever, forthwith.

"Where was May?" her mother was asking presently. Why, May was with her dear angels in the chancel, putting wreaths of primroses about their necks, standing there among them, in the rainbow shadows that struck down from the stained windows, and flecked the walls and pavement with varied jewels.

May was there among the angels, the fairest— a thousand times the fairest—of them all. It was from among the angels that charming Mrs Bethray took her home at last, when the jewels on wall and pavement had faded out, and the twilight came.

"You always liked those figures from a child," her mother said, " but you have finished now, I'm sure; tear yourself away from them, and come home to tea."

"Yes, I think I've finished with them for to-day," May answered, following her mother down the shady aisle, with a regretful glance behind. "Yes, I have finished for to-day; but I must soon be with them again. Do you know mother, being there amongst them to-day, brought back the old feeling I used to tell you

K

about when I was a child, a feeling that in those beautiful, calm, white faces there was always the faintest smile of welcome for me. Don't you recollect?"

"I remember all sorts of childish fancies of yours, May, heaps of them! See *how* well our hothouse flowers look, quite the best things here; Mrs Marfleet told me so just now."

They had approached Mrs Marfleet, who was busy with the font.

"Yes," she said, overhearing. "Decidedly the best. I am certain Modred will be charmed when he comes to-morrow, to see us put the finishing touches to everything. It is *very* good of you to help us so practically, Mrs Bethray"

Charming Mrs Bethray only smiled, bid mother and daughter good-night, and led May off, laughing, with an affectionate, motherly arm through hers. Indeed, May had never known her mother so affectionate, and would have been quite happy, save for the consciousness that there was that terrible conversation to come off that night. Even to talk of John Huson was painful and unpleasant to her. The ordeal was delayed as long as possible, for throughout dinner, and the evening that followed it, Mrs Bethray made no allusion to what was coming, and May naturally was not inclined to take the initiative.

But the time came at last.

"Where shall we have our little chat—down here or up by my bedroom fire, dearest?" charming Mrs Bethray asked, when May had played through her stock of valses, and sung one or two simple songs. "I suppose we *are* to have the chat? You remember the condition upon which I was going to let you off it?"

Poor little May, a shade paler than usual, but with the firm expression on her face again in an instant, laid a caressing hand upon her mother's shoulder, and replied,—

"Yes, I think we must have it mother. I am sure of it. Let us talk it over up by your bedroom fire. I like that room so much. I believe I learned and said my first words up there by that fire, didn't I?"

Mrs Bethray did not answer; with her arm

about her daughter's waist, she led her upstairs. She was meditating on the best way of playing that last card. She sat down in an easy-chair beside the blazing fire, as at that other interview in the drawing-room a few nights before, and May, drawing a footstool to her, seated herself at her feet—her old position there when she was a little child, she said.

She paused a moment, hoping her mother would begin; but charming Mrs Bethray was too good a diplomatist to do anything of the sort. Finding she remained silent, May began,—

"Well now, mother, about this affair—let us get it over and done with as quickly as possible. I think the best way, as it has clearly been a mistake all along, will be for me to send back the horse and phaeton, and give Mr Huson his ring when he comes to-morrow. That will be the best way, won't it?"

Charming Mrs Bethray, leaning back in her chair, with her eyes upon the fire and not upon the pretty, pleading face turned up to her, was silent a moment, and then said suddenly, with an appearance of the deepest sympathy,—

"Oh, May, how I wish we were free agents!
How I wish we *could* act like that! How I
wish, for your sake, that we could!"

"Oh, mother, mother! what *do* you mean?
Surely we *are* free agents in such a matter as
this!" May cried, turning very pale at the
sincere tone of sorrow in the words.

Charming Mrs Bethray had rehearsed this
scene a hundred times in her fancy, and it
was going exactly as she had always pictured
it. Following out her fancy rehearsals she
began to cry, silently, picturesquely, holding
four square inches of cambric and lace border
to her eyes, as was her custom at such
times.

"Yes," she said feebly through her tears,
"*you* are a free agent, May. *You* can refuse
him to-morrow as you wish. You can do it
easily; but you will sacrifice me—me, your
loving, affectionate mother, May. That is the
price at which you can avoid marrying John
Huson."

From behind the cambric skilfully held, Mrs
Bethray watched the effect of her words on

the innocent face before her, saw it change to terror and dismay, and shut it out with the cambric, satisfied.

"Sacrifice you? How can it do *that*, mother? Oh, I have always felt there was something behind all this terrible affair! *Do* tell me what it is? Do explain it, mother? You *know* I could not sacrifice you, that is, not if there was any possible way out of it. Oh, mother, think if there is no other way out of it than by my marrying Mr Huson! Think, mother!"

Charming Mrs Bethray, drying her eyes— which were not particularly wet—laid a hand upon May's head, and said, speaking very low,—

"May, in plain English, I am utterly and completely in Mr Huson's power. May, you know what I have told you he is, a financier. Their business is to lend money. Some time ago I was rash enough, mad enough, to borrow some of him; a great deal more than I can ever hope to repay. He could sell me up and ruin me, and you too, of course, utterly. at any moment. He has held his hand hitherto on *one*

condition. Oh, May! you can guess what that
condition is! You will not, you cannot see me
sacrificed!"

Yes! There, there, where she had taught
her her earliest words, this faded, worldly,
miserable doll, told her daughter this vile lie
—made this false appeal—to serve her own
basest ends! Told it, and made it with eyes
looking straight into the frank, truthful ones of
May, with her hand—a mother's hand—upon
May's golden head. Told it and made it, and
watched anxiously, critically, for the result of
her foul, debasing falsehood!

And May wavered awhile, uncertain how to
act; hesitated a moment, considering whether
she *could* sacrifice herself to save her mother.
And her mother saw the hesitation, and went
on.

"He is adamant, May! Positively adamant.
No pleading, no cajolery would be of the
slightest use—even from *you*. He has told me
so, often. He has pressed me, threatened me,
for this money, dozens of times. For a long
time I held out—for *your sake*. But then I

thought at last, as he was so rich—as a Rothschild or a Baring, you know—that perhaps—
perhaps for *my sake*, you would accept him.
Oh, May! think what I have suffered, and
try !"

"Oh, mother, mother! Why didn't you tell
me this *gradually*—long ago? Why didn't
you? And then I might have brought myself
to consider it. But it is so sudden—so dreadful—I don't know what to say!" And May
turned a dazed face to the fire, utterly confused and frightened.

"This place will be sold up May—and everything in it. I shall be turned homeless upon
the world. Think of it May!" her mother
pleaded.

It was a long, long struggle, which May—
poor little unfriended May—had with herself
there at her worthless mother's knee ; a long,
long struggle before she could cry out in a
broken voice,—

"I *will* try to think of it mother—I *will*
save you if I can. But it is terribly hard,
mother! Terribly hard! You've no idea *how*

hard it is mother!" And poor little May buried her head in her mother's lap and sobbed.

It might have moved any heart but the delicate one of charming Mrs Bethray. She merely asked her daughter to raise her head a moment, and when she did so, spread four square inches of pocket handkerchief over her knees, in case May's tears should spot the gown she was wearing, and looked at the fire over May's prostrate golden head with quiet satisfaction in her face. She was winning—fast!

May laid her head down again on the four square inches of lace-bordered cambric and sobbed on. Sobbed away all hope and all happiness, there, at her mother's feet. There, the one spot out of the whole world, where she had a right to expect help, and sympathy, and protection.

The moments went by, Time's sands running quickly, not a sparkling grain of them running out but some sparkling fancy, some bright, never-to-be-realised hope of May's ran out with it.

And Laura Bethray still looked quietly, above the lowered golden head, at the fire, and saw success there; once, thinking of Roland Vance's last letter upstairs, she smiled.

Childish days, sparkling girlhood, high hopes for the future — one by one May sobbed them all away there, at her mother's knee, that night.

When the first fury of the storm had swept across her, and she rose pale, and heavy-eyed, there was nothing of the bright, happy girlish May remaining—she had sobbed *that* all away. Throughout the night, after she had parted with her mother, and received her mother's kiss as her reward, she lay awake, watching the glittering stars and driving clouds, seeing in them—in the whole future before her — a dreariness and despair she had never dreamed before.

"If I could *only* die! If I could *only* die!" The poor child sobbed, oh, how often, through that dawnless night!

And all that night the little trickling brook dripped into the silver mirror; and all that night tears fell from the bright eyes that had so often been reflected there, as fast—a tear for every drop.

So the old days, and thoughts, and hopes for which she cared to live, vanished out May Bethray's life. She wept them all away that night.

CHAPTER THE THIRTEENTH.

John Huson arrived at the Grange at his usual time—an hour before dinner. He was not altogether satisfied with the state of affairs with regard to May On his previous visit he had hinted as much to charming Mrs Bethray, and she had laughed it off as well as she could, on the plea of her daughter's youth and coyness.

"That's it you know," she said, "only that. She quite considers herself engaged, I assure you."

But John Huson wasn't exactly the sort of person with whom it was easy to laugh anything off. The bull-dog element in his nature —the element that made him what he was— precluded that.

"I'm a business man, you know," he replied

gravely "I like to see exactly what I am doing. I like to have everything in which I engage closely defined. I wish you would speak to her and see whether she detests me very much indeed. If so, it would be outrageous to proceed further in the matter. Even a business man, Mrs Bethray, is not wholly lost to all feelings of compassion; it would be terrible to force the girl into accepting me!"

It was this speech that made charming Mrs Bethray tremble for the result of her scheme; made her see that her highest card must be played without hesitation.

"Oh, don't be so silly!" she said airily. "You men never understand the signs of a woman's heart! Never! All this coolness of hers is the strongest point in your favour. Can't you see that? But as you wish for something more tangible, ask her plainly next Saturday when you come, and judge for yourself by her reply. You know, in spite of her gay manner, she's a girl who wouldn't throw herself at a man's head. No girl at that age will. When she accepts you on Saturday, she'll probably do it very quietly ; but *I know her,* and if she *does,* take my word for it that it proves she's very much attached to you."

So John Huson had stepped into the brougham, waiting to take him to the station that Monday morning, and driven away.

Charming Mrs Bethray chances to be in the hall this particular Saturday, when the financier drives up to the door in the neat little brougham. She welcomes him cordially,—

" Oh, John ! I'm so glad you've got here in time for dinner, with all this extra Easter-holiday traffic, I was very doubtful about your doing so. Come into the library a moment. I've something to say to you."

John Huson follows her into the named room, making only a subdued reply to her effusive greeting. Reading people pretty closely, this gilt-edged volume rather sickens him.

" I've some news for you," she says, leaning a hand upon his shoulder. " I told you last week to ask her in so many words to-day— didn't I ? "

John Huson merely bowed.

"Very well. Now, I can tell you beforehand what her answer will be, though please remember I told you last week. She will say 'Yes.' They're such little dissemblers at seventeen, John (you see I already take the liberty of using your Christian name), such fearful little dissemblers, John. I recollect I was just the same—exactly. She'll accept you very coldly, I shouldn't wonder—but never mind. I had a private little chat with her last night—such a cosy chat! She quite opened her heart to me, as people say. *If* you could only have been behind a curtain, or in one of the cupboards, John, you'd have—well, it isn't fair to tell you anything further—it positively isn't. Only, if she's cool to you when you speak to her, remember what I say. They are all dissemblers, John—everyone. And now, having fulfilled my mission, I'll leave you to smoke that small cigar you're dying for, I know;" and with a playful kissing of her hand to him, charming Mrs Bethray goes out of the library gaily, humming a tune. But the tune gets rather out of harmony as she goes upstairs to her bedroom, her head is so full of a fact she keeps telling herself over and over again: "I did it beautifully, with scarcely a *white one*, even."

May spent that whole Saturday in a bitter, determined struggle with herself, walking about the shrubbery paths, pausing often beside the stile, and trying to realise it all. She never once thought of doubting her mother's word. Far too truthful herself for that, she believed it all—the whole vile lie charming Mrs Bethray told her. She was only seventeen: most things told as true *are* so at seventeen.

Looking at it a thousand ways, and seeing only the one awful way out of it, with tears and agony unspeakable, May decided to save her mother, and sacrifice herself. But it was terrible to her—in spite of the sleepless night she had passed—trying to realise it. The prayer she had prayed so often throughout that night was on her lips a thousand times all day: "Oh, that I might die! oh, that I only might!"

Everything about her seemed to have found a voice to tell her misery; the breeze sighed it, the birds sang it, the dripping of the little brook was tears indeed.

It was coming into the house by a side doorway that she met Mews, stout and quiet, and kindly as ever. Something in that face she remembered so well in childhood, had an irresistible attraction for her; somehow it seemed the only thing unchanged in her misery.

"Oh, Mews!" she exclaimed, throwing her arms about the old woman's neck. "Oh, Mews! do you remember one day—a month or two ago—I told you—how happy I was? Do you Mews?"

Mews with a kindly hand upon the golden head seeking her shoulder for consolation, said she did, perfectly.

"Yes, Mews, and so do I—and now—I should like to tell you how—but it's no good, Mews —not a bit."

Where was the old gladsome May, for this was a new, broken-hearted, sobbing one, whose tears fell fast upon the housekeeper's ample shoulder.

L

No wonder that Saturday's dinner is rather a dreary affair, in spite of all charming Mrs Bethray's efforts to the contrary.

"Of course, you're going on Monday, the last day of the season?" she asks towards dessert; hoping by the favourite theme to start a conversation, and trying to look fondly at her daughter, as she puts the question.

"I don't think I shall, mother; I don't care for it."

"I think I shall finish with them," John Huson says quietly.

"Why, of course you will! you've already promised to stay Monday night here, and I'm certain you wouldn't require that large portmanteau I saw in the corridor, if it wasn't to hold your hunting things."

"Yes; I have brought them, and my horse is coming down Monday by the special. I hope we shall have a fine day"

It seems like some preposterous dream to May as she hears. Fancy caring about the weather, with such a load as her heart bears! Why, she would welcome the end of the world gladly if it would but come. The thought of *how* gladly, almost makes her smile in her misery She is haunted by the dread of the impending moment that shall see her fate sealed, past all hope of reprieve: almost longs it may come soon and be done with. How long will she be able to keep her resolution if it is delayed?

And careless of the misery she has brought upon her child, charming Mrs Bethray laughs and talks in the highest spirits, for she knows the game is won.

When the mother, and the daughter she is selling into bondage for the serving of the basest end, go into the drawing-room, and are alone together, the former slips an arm about May's waist and kisses her, and says,—

"Darling, you're the best girl in the world, and I love you *very* dearly!"

And May, disengaging herself quickly as she can, cries out in such a tone of agony, as even startles charming Mrs Bethray,—

"Don't speak to me, mother, for Heaven's sake, if I am to do it! Pray don't. I can't bear it. I really can't, you don't know—you never *will* know—what I am doing for your sake; if you speak another word, I shall shriek."

Charming Mrs Bethray (with a passing glance at the set of her gown in a neighbouring mirror) thinks it discreet to leave the room, and so doing, encounters John Huson in the hall. With a meaning smile, she asks him,—

"*Am* I not considerate to write three letters upstairs in my room, and so leave the coast clear for you? Do you think you really deserve it?" and passes on upstairs, kissing her hand in an airy farewell to him.

May is standing by the fire, looking down into it, with one hand upon the marble of the mantel-shelf, when he enters the room. It is a blazing fire, for the spring evening's are chilly, and the flames paint a ruddy glow on everything within their range, save one—the beautiful white face looking down into them. The ruddiest glow that ever was could not glamour *that.* So pale, so sad, it might belong to one of the angels in the chancel of Fairacre Church.

John Huson, coming up behind her, does not see the full misery of it. He only sees the lithe figure that he loves in strong relief against a fiery background, and it makes his heart beat faster.

"May," he says in a wonderfully softened voice. "May—I think it is time we should come to some better understanding—you and I. What I am, you know—a plain business man. But I have a heart, May—and that is wholly yours—I am much older than you, of course; but I sha'n't be too strict. You shall do just as you like, May, in all your pleasures— I have more money than you will ever want to spend—you shall have all you wish for in that way—I'm not terribly bad tempered—and —that's about all, May. I'm very plain and business-like with you, you see — I can't help it—it's my nature. I want you to say that you will marry me — I want you to say 'Yes.'"

He has slipped his arm round her waist, and he feels her tremble. He has placed his face very close to hers, and he sees her lips move inarticulately—but he thinks they whisper the word he wants most to hear.

"Never mind about *saying* it," he says kindly, thinking of her mother's words that night, "never mind about *saying* it, see here! I am going to take this little hand prisoner—if you don't remove it I shall understand."

He takes the marble hand and presses it. She lets it rest with him silently.

"You have made me so happy, May!" he says feelingly. "Do say *one* word, dearest?"

"I'm glad—I've—made anybody happy," a little forlorn voice answers him, and before he can detain her, she has hurried from the room.

She meets her mother in the corridor upstairs, and dashes past her with a scared face and a gesture that precludes a word on charming Mrs Bethray's part; she speeds into her own little room, locks the door behind her, throws herself upon her bed, and repeats that new prayer that has come lately and supplanted all her old ones,—

"Oh, that I might die! Oh! that I only might!"

Downstairs Mrs Bethray is congratulating John Huson upon his formal engagement.

"Never mind her being cool, John! Remember what I told you before dinner—they're such fearful dissemblers at seventeen! I was just the same—exactly *then!*"

And the happy mother insists on following her son-in-law-that-is-to-be into the library, that he "may have some one to smoke his cigar at," as she puts it, in the highest of high spirits.

She has won!

CHAPTER THE FOURTEENTH.

DAZED and miserable, feeling hopelessly lost to the world for ever, poor little May passed a dreary, confused Easter Sunday. An impenetrable wall seemed to have risen up around her life, and shut out all the brightness of it. Nothing that could happen, good or ill, mattered to her; it was all the same. A dreary future, shadowed by intangible fears, stretched away in front of her, and the thought of it weighed like lead upon her heart.

She went to church. Charming Mrs Bethray and John Huson went too, but she was silent there and back, dreaming all through the service, with eyes upon the marble angels in the chancel, and scarcely seeing them. At luncheon she was still silent, and shadowy fears crossed her mother's mind as she noticed John Huson's attention fixed closely on the pale, drooping flower, all freshest life so short a while ago.

They sat over the drawing-room fire in the twilight a long time that evening, all three of them, nobody speaking much, for the heart of each was full.

Presently, charming Mrs Bethray, hoping to start a conversation, tries her usual subject under such circumstances.

"Have you noticed the sunset to-night? A glorious day to-morrow for the last run of the season. You had better go, May, it will do you good."

"I don't think I care to go, mother," May answers with her eyes dreamily upon the coals in the deepening dusk.

"I really wish you would; we always get such a good run from the Thicket," John Huson says kindly. "If it wouldn't bore you very much, I wish you would go with me, May. The going is excellent, and Black Diamond will be very fresh. Think of the gallop across

Boyne Park; we are sure to uncart in Boyne Park; think of the turf there, May!"

Apparently May does think of it, and the old enthusiasm for her favourite sport comes back to her as she does so, for her face suddenly brightens, and she looks round the room with the expression of one waking out of some terrible opiate dream. A new light is in her eyes, a new colour in her face, at the very idea of that gallop, and she answers quite briskly,—

"Oh! if you wish it, *as* you wish it, I will go to-morrow. Black Diamond *will* be fresh no doubt," and then, as though the momentary excitement had passed, she leans back in her chair again, silent; very silent—silent all the remainder of the evening.

Somehow, in the saying of good-night all round, John Huson and Mrs Bethray find themselves left alone together. The financier seizes the opportunity, and says seriously,—

"Mrs Bethray, I am still doubtful of this step I am taking. May's manner is very strange and quiet I am going to ask you a question, Mrs Bethray."

"Oh, of course! What is it?"

"It is this: do you know, do you think it possible, that your daughter has some prior attachment? I don't wish to hint such a thing to *her* if I can help it; you must know. I read people, Mrs Bethray; as a business man it is necessary I should do so, very often I have suspicions. Please consider carefully before your answer. Do you think it possible her heart is already bestowed?"

"My dear John!" exclaims Laura, laying a hand affectionately on his shoulder, "how terribly jealous you lovers are! I can *assure* you her heart is only yours. But, John! remember what I told you, they are such *fearful* dissemblers at seventeen!"

And John, not quite liking it all, is obliged to be satisfied.

May is up very early that soft spring Easter morning; has written a sad little letter to Charles Darrac, telling him that for her mother's sake she must give him up for ever. Will explain all if she ever sees him again; has been out for a stroll through the shrubberies, and stood a long time beside the silver mirror and the falling brook—has done all this—done it very tearfully; and come into the breakfast-room first after all.

John Huson looks really very well in his black and white costume (he has too good taste to assume pink), and is very cheery over his meal. Before it is finished, his horse appears outside the breakfast-room windows, led by the neatest of grooms.

May is already in her habit, and running upstairs to fit on her hat, meets Mews in the corridor, and hugs her with something of her old cheeriness of manner.

"You know how fond I am of you," she says, going lightly down the dark oak stairs again, with her habit draped from her hand. She bids her mother a rapid adieu, for the horses are impatient, and then John Huson and the girl he loves are walking their hunters down the avenue, side by side. May looks back at the lodge gates, and waves a last farewell to Mrs Bethray, who is standing in a rather studied attitude of grace upon the steps of the glass-fitted porchway entrance.

Half-an-hour later, John Huson sits upon that wonderful hunter of his in Boyne Park, looking with pride at the golden-haired girl beside him.

Well he may! Amongst all that gay throng waiting there on the verdant turf for the hounds to come up, there is not one fairer or better mounted. And in May's face is almost happiness, as her glance rests upon that spot in the sunk fence, a quarter of a mile ahead, where the stag made a bold spring for liberty and the plough, and vanished ten minutes ago.

John Huson is off his horse, taking up a link in his curb chain, when the hounds come up, spread out like a fan, pick up the scent, and speed away over the grass silently as a dream.

"Don't wait for me, you know the gate to the left," he calls out in the excitement of the moment, for his horse is impatient, and it delays his mounting for half a minute. "Don't wait, I'll overtake you at the gate."

But May has not waited, she is already a hundred yards away, for Black Diamond is fresh, and pulling hard.

John Huson is in his saddle, turns his horse towards the well-known gate, when an exclamation from some of the numerous crowd of spectators, makes him alter his direction, with a sudden fear at his heart, as he speeds away as fast as that three - hundred guinea hunter can carry him.

The whole field is making for the gate, the only outlet in the required direction—for the sunk fence is eighteen feet wide, with a drop into a boggy willow-bordered waste. The whole field thunders towards the gate, with one exception, and that one exception is May Bethray, who rides resolutely, alone with the flying pack, straight towards the fence.

John Huson gallops after her and shouts a caution, but it is useless: straight toward those yawning eighteen feet, straight towards that boggy landing May rides, heedless of everything. The hounds, fifty yards ahead of her, struggle down out of sight, and reappear in the furtherside water meadow, speeding like birds upon the wing! Black Diamond pricks her ears, measures the distance, and goes straight at it desperately, all her aristocratic blood at fever-heat. John Huson, feeling sick and giddy as he rides at racing speed after the girl he loves, sees the black horse with her golden burthen gather herself for the effort, make a brave attempt—land—struggle—take one stride—nearly recover, and then roll over and disappear from sight.

What has happened he cannot tell, he only knows that there is no way of reaching May save by the gate half-a-mile off, or by following across that sunken fence. John Huson is no coward, and he is not an instant making his decision. With his teeth close set, and all the bull-dog in his nature at its strongest, he takes hold of his horse as he has never done before, and sends him at it. He nears it at racing speed, sees in the last stride Black Diamond on her feet looking wildly at the little prostrate figure on the ground, knows no more till he is on his knees beside that little figure,

imploring it to speak—but one word, and meeting only an awful silence.

A crowd soon collects, and they carry her—
the lightest burthen that ever was—to a neighbouring farm house, and lay her down tenderly
upon a dimity curtained bed upstairs.

Two doctors are in attendance — sprung
from nowhere—instantly, and for some awful
moments are left alone with the unconscious
figure by their own desire.

"Who is this young lady's friend?" asks one
of them presently, a florid man, looking very
grave.

"I am. What is the matter — she is not
dead?" Huson answers in a broken voice.

"Come in here," the doctor says quietly,
leading the way into a small farm sitting-room
and closing the door behind them.

"Well?" Huson inquires, when they are alone
"Well?"

"I have bad news for you, I regret to say—
the worst news—are you prepared for it?"

"Oh, my God! She is not dead?"

"No. She is almost conscious again, but, in

fact, there are internal injuries—the gravest. I may tell you plainly there is no hope—none at all. Fortunately, we think she will experience very little pain ; there are no bones broken —not one."

"Will you fetch her mother. May I ask you to do that, and at once," John Huson says with something of his cold business promptitude upon him. "And when may I see Miss Bethray ? "

"My colleague will fetch you. I will go for her mother," the doctor says. " Where will you be ? "

" Here," the other man replies in a constrained voice, and so is left alone with his sorrow.

He is a wonderfully changed man, when, in response to the other doctor's summons, he comes softly into the room where May lies upon the dimity hung bed. With amazing gentleness he draws the dimity aside, and looks down lovingly upon the little white face lying there looking up at his with a new expression he has never seen there before.

"My dear, are you in pain ? "

"No, not exactly pain, you know, but very ill—very strange. I think I am going to die —I really do." Her voice fades to a whisper; and John Huson, man of the world — cold-hearted as many say, moves to the window and looks out at the sunny landscape, with tears coursing rapidly down his cheeks: she is very dear to him.

Presently her voice recalls him to her side. Controlling his face as best he can, he takes one of the little icy hands in his, and says, "Yes, darling!"

"Are we alone?"

"Perfectly" (For the doctor has considerately left the room.)

"Then, I want to ask you something—a favour. Will you promise it to me?"

"Yes, yes. Whatever it is."

"Then, about mother, you won't let this— this accident—alter anything. You won't press her for the money, will you? I *was* going to marry you. I had promised, you know."

She looks up at him pleadingly, with glance and words straight from her heart.

In that glance, and in those words he reads it all; reads the vileness of the scheming, miserable woman, who had sold her daughter by a lie—for gold.

"I promise, dearest—solemnly—but tell me—I was going to ask you the same question once yesterday, May. I read people quickly, you know. You never really and truly loved me, you loved someone else—tell me who, that I may send for him now?"

She does not answer for a moment—she cannot—but she takes his hand and presses it to her lips.

"Oh, how good you are!" she exclaims feebly; then, "oh, how good you are!" And he knows what those words, so spoken, mean.

"Whom shall I send for?" he says, almost whispering.

There is no need for her to answer, at that moment the door is hurriedly thrown open, and a man comes in, pale as the little figure on the bed, and the look in that little figure's face, tells John Huson there's no need to send for anyone. He takes one of the white hands and kisses it reverently, fondly, and then, with averted face, and in silence, goes out.

His part is played.

Darrac flings himself upon his knees beside the bed, and buries his face in its coverings, speechless—sobbing.

Then a little voice, a ghost of its old gay self, but a recognisable ghost all the same, says,—

"Why, Poet, poor Poet—not tears? Why have *you* come—how have you come?"

"Oh, my God! how can I tell you? my darling, my life. I came—came happily—until I heard of *this*—came happily—"

"Not happily—not happily, Charley; you must not forget the uncle—the impediment you know."

"Oh! May, darling May, he—I *cannot* say it—" and Charles Darrac breaks off sobbing again.

"He, what? please tell me, I should like to know. *please?*"

"He saw your letter, May, he *would* read it, and—and—he was so pleased, he told me to come up and tell you he gave his consent. Oh!

May, dearest May! can you not get better? *can* you not, May?"

"No, Charley," she whispers faintly, kissing him softly again and again. "No, Charley, I'm afraid I can't."

He holds her in his arms, imploringly covers her face and brow with passionate, unavailing kisses. Even while he holds her with a grasp to baffle cold Death himself, a faintness comes upon her, but she struggles bravely with it, struggles to say a few more words, and when she can, they are about Black Diamond.

"I don't think she's hurt, Charley, I give her to you—remember. And Charley" (very faintly now), "Charley, it was my fault, all mine. She didn't bolt, as Mr Huson thinks. I rode her at it Charley, on purpose. I told you once that when I was tired of my life I would. I *was* tired of it this morning. But, Charley, don't let Mr Huson know I did it, please. Let him think Black Diamond bolted. I would rather he thought that."

She lay silent for a moment or two in his arms, and then, with a sudden start asked,—

"Where is mother—I want to see mother?"

Where *is* charming Mrs Bethray? She is fainting quietly and picturesquely at home, on receipt of the doctor's intelligence: worthy of nothing better.

"Charley—is it getting dark? Charley—I always loved you—though I used to tease you. And you're very clever, Charley, and you'll be very famous one day—and then—you won't forget your little Daisy—you won't, will you, Charley—even if you *are* the Laureate?"

"I shall never, never forget you darling—never!"

"I believe you—I *do* love you, Charley—hold me tighter, Charley—"

It is the last word upon her innocent lips—the last word upon them when the darkness comes.

And the moral?

The moral lies with several of our characters: With John Huson, going back to the world a softened man—with nearly all the bull-dog in his nature dead. John Huson giving the three thousand pounds to the woman he most loathes on earth, because of his promise to the little girl he loved.

With the cold, distant, awe-inspiring Poet of years to come ; rich and famous, launching the fieriest darts of that gift in which he excels all other living rhymers from time to time upon an intently listening world ; a world to which he is cold and careless ; a man to whom his gold and fame are nothing : a stern man, who lays aside all his sternness often when alone beside the silver mirror and the falling brook of Holly-bush stile—lays it aside, and cries out in his undying agony,—

" Oh, my darling ! my darling ! why were you taken from me ? "

Yes, the moral lies with anyone save charming Mrs Bethray She is only grieved, and deeply, too, at the falsity of Roland Vance, who took the money she had paid so high a price for, and disappeared forthwith — leaving all his debts unpaid.

No moral lies with charming Mrs Bethray, none at all. She is only sad about Roland

Vance, and very, *very* angry. She has learned
no lesson. Is as vain and foolish as ever. She
will sell the Grange to Charles Darrac, and at
a figure far above its worth. But he *will* have
it at any price: Hollybush stile is on the
property Charming Mrs Bethray is looking out
for a snug little house in Town; and meanwhile, she has the warmest sympathy and moral
support in all trials from the Revd. Modred
and Mrs Marfleet.

It wasn't more than a year afterwards; they
had again taken the stag on the outskirts of a
Buckinghamshire village, and the usual varied
field was straggling off homewards. As once
before, Farmer Brown and Farmer Harris rode
amicably side by side in wake of the company.
As before, there was a clear sky betokening
frost, and Farmer Brown, with a weatherwise
eye upon it, sees a little twinkling star that
has come out early. Still keeping his eye somewhere up there, he says in rather a trembling
voice,—

"Do you mind a year ago, Harris, when we

took the stag here, and *she* was cut—poor little thing: she as was took, as I may say, by an early frost? Do 'ee Harris?"

"Uncommon well, Brown—"

"And do 'ee see that theer star a-shining up theer?"

"Uncommon plain, Brown."

"And has it ever come to you, Harris, looking at the like, as *she's* up theer, with the angels?"

"It has, Brown, uncommon often; and whenever it *do* so come, and I think of her, with her golden hair and her bright eyes, up among them angels, and cherubims and what-nots, it *do* seem to me, Brown, as there ain't one of 'em—not in all the glittering lot—as is purer, or brighter, or more lovelier than what she is!"

THE END.

AN AWKWARD AFFAIR.

AN AWKWARD AFFAIR,

BEING AN INCIDENT IN THE LIFE OF A MAN
WHO MIGHT HAVE BEEN WISER.

———◆———

CHAPTER THE FIRST.

GEORGY HAWKES called it a "bit of a sell,"
but I prefer the above title for a short account
of the incident in question. If there should be
any stray reader who has a dim belief that the
quality known as "heart" is deficient among
women, what follows will banish the dimness,
and strengthen the belief, amazingly.

The date of the incident was ten years ago.
A page will frame the picture, and then the looking at it will rest with the readers of the succeed-

ing chapters, which are all short. Perhaps the readers won't get quite the same light upon the canvas that I do; assuredly it won't affect them as it affected me. Now for the frame. I, James Stewart, was twenty-five, a sufficiently rich bachelor, residential owner of an old Elizabethan house, known as Brandon Manor, in Beechshire. Both parents dead; a dear old aunt keeping house for me, and, as a companion of the sager sort, the Reverend William Wade, an innocent old man who was once my tutor. Nobody very knowable within reach of the Manor save a family named Hawkes, settled a few years earlier in the village. Hawkes *père*, who was in some vague and shadowy way connected with the city, took a place in the country to correct a certain bad habit, which had arisen from conviviality and dry sherry. Somehow the remedy had an adverse effect upon the disease. Mr Hawkes went about in a chronic state of inviting people to "take a glass of dry sherry," and, as people didn't respond so readily as might have been expected, he, like every honourable physician, was quite ready to take his own medicine. It may have been the doing of this which led to Mr Hawkes being somewhat incoherent in his talk sometimes.

There were only two girls by way of family, "Georgy" and Eva. They were, from the first, like sisters to me. Indeed, the younger one, "Georgy," tried, in the early days of our acquaintaince, to be something more than a sister; but as I did not view the matter in quite the same light, we soon settled down into the sisterly state, and all went well.

The Hawkes girls liked private theatricals: I got up private theatricals at the Manor. They were pronounced such a brilliant success, that our dear old vicar, Mr Primrose, asked me as a favour to produce them at the village schools in aid of his "Organ Fund," or something musical and charitable of that sort. This I did, and the proceeds were so satisfactory that Primrose hinted "something of the same sort three months later" would be most acceptable—for the "Clothing Club," I fancy. To this I also agreed; and I have often since wondered whether people wearing clothes paid

for by those theatricals felt anything remarkable about the garments. They *should* have
done so, for those second theatricals were very
fateful.

So much for the frame.

CHAPTER THE SECOND.

IT is impossible to tell what a woman may be up to.

I have the very strongest belief in the truth of that line. The youngest of the Hawkes girls and the one who, I have told you, would, in the early days of our friendship, have been even more than a sister to me, was always called "Georgy"; her real name being Georgina. This young lady seemed to have forgotten all about those early days of our friendship, and to have settled now into a very nice sisterly girl. Had I guessed that it was otherwise, I should have been more careful than I was. But it is a mistake to anticipate anything in this world, even in the telling of a story, so we must proceed in due order and gradually.

N

The clothing club theatricals were close at hand: to come off privately at the Manor, with a dance afterwards, and the following night to take place publicly at the school, on the first of August.

I had been in town for a few weeks as usual at that season, and had left in the middle of July to attend rehearsals; thoroughly hard we worked at them, too. The piece—I forget the name at the moment—was a comedy of some sort, and, rashly enough, I played the part of husband to Georgy Hawkes. It was an uncommonly foolish thing to do under all the circumstances; but I liked the character, suspected no evil, and the piece went capitally in rehearsal.

I had been out one day, a week before the date of the private representation, and, coming home about five, went to the morning-room, knowing that my aunt and Mr Wade would be having their afternoon tea together there. They were. My aunt was entrenched behind the little tea-table. She had white hair, a kindly face, and a sweet temper, the last two being very rare qualities in any old maid. Poor old Wade (white hair and soft, pleasant voice) was sitting at a little distance from her.

The summer sunshine, streaming through the old mullioned windows, seemed to linger upon those two grey heads lovingly, corroborating what they were agreeing together, viz., that:

"It was a remarkably bright, happy, beautiful world if people would only believe so much; only a diseased mind could see in it anything else."

"It has *some* dark spots on it, though, surely," I say, chiming into the conversation.

"Men may sometimes bring trouble to themselves and others by their ambition or their avarice," Wade answers. "But then, to counteract all sorrow, we have pure, innocent, guileless woman sent to cheer our path, and guide us to happiness."

"Exactly *my* view of the matter," my aunt said placidly.

I never knew those two disagree on any point; but then they were single. Had they been man and wife, and I have not the least doubt they would have quarrelled fearfully, and, sooner or later, have applied for a divorce.

I sat down and took my cup of tea, wondering whether it would be wise to cite a few contrary experiences that had come under my own personal observation, and was just deciding to leave the worthy old people to their own undisturbed belief, when my butler, Philips (irreverently named "The Bishop," from his general appearance and solemnity), announced "The Misses Hawkes."

The two girls sure enough—Georgy and Eva; both very well dressed, and not at all distasteful objects to look upon.

"How do you do, Prince? That's an original question, by-the-bye, isn't it?" Georgy says, sitting down within easy reach of the cake tray, and helping herself to the best slice.

Both the girls nicknamed me "Prince" within six weeks of our knowing each other. Seeing that Eva was more diffident as to the tea-tray, I got up and attended to her wants as best I could, making a civil reply to Georgy the while.

My poor aunt was always terribly afraid of
the girls, and Mr Wade invariably more or less
nervous in their company.

"Tell you why we came," Georgy went on
presently (helping herself to an additional lump
of sugar, with a nod to my aunt by way of
apology). "Tell you why we came. I want a
card for a friend for this night week. It's a
woman; knows a lot about acting, and likes
it; *has* acted privately often. She'll stop with
us for a week. Are the cards in your writing-
table drawer in the library? If so, I'll go and
fetch one."

These Hawkes girls usually have it all their
own way with me, and I go to fetch the card
myself.

"You fill it in," Georgy says, when I return.

"Such a joke, as you've never seen her."

I don't quite perceive the joke, but I take a
pen and ask the name.

"Edith Grenville."

I write it down, and hand the card to Miss
Hawkes without a word.

"You must be careful of your heart," Eva

says, speaking for the first time. "Edith is very dangerous."

There is something in the voice that makes me look at the speaker. I am rather amused, as I do so, to notice that she is regarding me with a glance of evident pity. I don't in the least understand it all, but the tea goes on cheerfully enough, and Georgy helps herself again, this time to the best of a little dish of peaches on the small tea-table.

"Beautiful peaches," she says, "better than ours by a long way. Have one, Eva."

I add my entreaties, and Eva *does* have one. She is not quite so pushing as Georgy.

"Prince," the latter says, when they are standing up before their departure, "we're walking home—come that far with us; we'll post this letter on the way. Give me an envelope—I'll address it. Got a stamp?"

Of course I've got a stamp, and so I give it her.

"The post-office is out of our way," she says, after dashing off an address, whilst sticking the envelope together, "and if we take it home, our post-bag will be gone."

Her eyes rest upon dear old Wade as she speaks.

"I am now going to the post," he says softly. "Let me take your note; I have several others to post."

She gives him her missive. Of course she meant him to make the offer when she spoke.

I go towards Brandon House with the girls. Chancing to look back in the Manor avenue, Wade is visible toddling along in a contrary direction with the letters.

I have often speculated as to what he thought about as he went to post with that card. Whether the winds said anything, or the clouds *looked* anything, on his journey; I daresay they didn't.

It was a fine evening, and everything was at its best. A pheasant got up quite close to us at the end of the home plantation, and went off as lazily as though aware that the first of October was more than two months distant

"I shall see you to-morrow," Georgy says, when I leave them at the lodge (it is too near dinner time for me to go in, though they press me to do so — Eva quietly, Georgy effusively).

"Oh, yes, the rehearsal," I say abstractedly, for I am thinking of something else.

"Before that, I fancy," replies Georgy. "I'm going to fish your lake to-morrow. I believe it wants stocking again, I haven't caught much there lately."

I am no fisherman, and this is probably true. Promise made for re-stocking forthwith.

I walk home quickly in the early twilight, smoking a cigar which Georgy has insisted upon lighting for me.

CHAPTER THE THIRD.

THE theatricals were a great success, everybody said so. There was no hitch from first to last, and the prompter's post was a sinecure.

Leaving the stage hurriedly when the curtain fell for the last time, I made a bolt upstairs to exchange the costume of the piece for the more ordinary evening dress of civilised man in this nineteenth century.

Descending again, I made my way to the identical library in which I now write these words, as the majority of the guests were assembled there, waiting my advent to go in to supper.

Men are usually quicker with their changes of apparel than women; but on this particular occasion Georgy had beaten me, and there she was, just inside the door, waiting with the rest of the company.

She made for me at once.

"Come along, Prince," she said—I won't swear she didn't take my arm, to facilitate my movements—"I want to introduce you to Edith Grenville."

The next moment we were standing before a lady who had her back to a lamp, and was consequently in shadow.

"Mr Stewart—Miss Grenville."

Miss Grenville bows—I do the same. It is all very hurried, for an important dowager is already frowning at me for not taking her in to supper sooner. I hardly notice Edith Grenville at all. If I had never seen her again, I should have had no idea of her appearance, save that she was tall, with a good figure; I saw that much.

Supper was soon over, and we commenced dancing.

My duty dances over, I sought out the stranger. Crossing the hall, I came upon Wade. How it chanced that he was not in bed, or praying for our immortal souls (his usual custom on such occasions, I believe, for he disapproved of theatricals), I have never been able to discover; as it was, he came up to me at once.

"James," he said, with more animation than I had ever seen him betray previously. "James, what have I often told you?"

"Really—" I began, when he interrupted me.

"That women are angels, and you have laughed at me. Now, come here."

With a vague idea that my poor dear old tutor had been supping not wisely but too well, I followed him in silence through the crowded room to the open doors leading to a conservatory.

Here, drawing aside the heavy curtains festooning the doorway, we paused.

"Look!" he said softly, and I looked.

A large Chinese lantern, suspended from the centre dome, threw a soft but sufficient light upon tall branching ferns, on many coloured foliage, and on—something else!

Seated on a low couch, and alone—utterly alone, was—it is absurd to try and describe her, she was simply the most beautiful woman I have ever seen. Face and figure were equally perfect. Rather over than under medium size, with dark hair curling closely about her head; with a pensive expression upon her face, and her hands opening and closing her fan indolently, with a hundred other charms impossible of description, she might have turned any man's head anywhere. But there—with a sparkling fountain beside her, with unhackneyed foliage all around, and the strains of a dreamy valse in the perfumed air—she was divine.

There is a lot in association!

"Who is it?" I asked in a whisper; for the vision took my breath away.

"Miss Grenville," Wade replied, in the same low tone.

Next instant I was oblivious of Wade; oblivious of everything save that I was sitting on the couch beside Edith Grenville; that she was looking at me, sometimes speaking to me; whilst I was talking some sufficiently incoherent words about a confounded tree-fern, of which she was particularly anxious to know the name.

For a long time I never thought of asking her to dance. I was far too dazed and dazzled to think of such a thing. Occasionally faces appeared and disappeared in the distant doorway of the conservatory. Once, I know, I saw Georgy's face there, with a look upon it I can remember even now: a strange expression, in which sorrow, malice, and joy were all inexplic-'ably mingled and co-mingled.

I can recall very little of that conversation. To the best of my belief it centred almost, if not entirely, on the tree-fern. (That identical tree-fern is living now, and I never pass it without an impossible sensation that somehow it has got the better of me: it is so utterly untouched by time.)

"Won't you give me a dance, Miss Grenville?" I say presently, with difficulty persuading myself that I am awake.

"Do you know, I don't often dance. I had just as soon sit here."

"Won't you dance *once?*" I plead.

"If you really *wish* it, with pleasure," rising and placing her hand through my arm.

I don't know what the dance was; a "square," I think, for I recollect, in the fashion of the time, Edith wore ribbon bows, with little fluttering ends upon her arm, and that one of those bows slipped down to her wrist in the progress of the dance, and, laughing, she asked me to replace it (what a beautiful white rounded arm that was, too!), and I know we were standing still at the moment. Yes it must have been a "square," for I distinctly remember now, that as we "set," Edith was asking me whether a high temperature was necessary for the well-being of tree-ferns; and if it were possible to propagate by breaking a piece off one.

"Possible to break a piece off!" Why, I would have broken a piece off my heart willingly and given her, if she fancied it, only she had the whole of it already! Usually, I believe, I was considered a good host; that night I was the worst ever created!

Directly after the dance we went back to the conservatory; but, alas! another couple were in possession of our former seat! However, it didn't matter in the least; Edith mentioned that she thought the artistic effect of a house, *seen from the outside,* when lighted up, was *so* good! There was a terrace on two sides of the manor, and taking a shawl (goodness knows whose!) I muffled her up, and we were out on that terrace in no time.

There was a faint crescent moon, and the park lay in a silent, silver mist. There is a lot in association!

Suddenly I burst my tree-fern bonds, and quoted a line of poetry! (I am inclined to fancy wrongly.) But if ever a poetic quotation could be pardoned, I claim that favour for that act on such a night, with such a woman!

Edith laughed—a little, quiet musical laugh.

"You are poetical, Mr Stewart," she said.

"You *can't* imply that you are *not*," I exclaimed fervidly. I've no doubt she thought me a fool; I believe any exhibition of "soul" meets that reception from her sex. For woman is far, far more practical than man.

"I'm afraid I'm not *very* poetical," she answered, smiling still. She had the most wonderful teeth when she smiled that I ever saw. "To show

how practical I am," she went on, "I'll ask you
if you don't think you ought to be paying
more attention to your friend Georgy?"

"I think she's quite capable of taking care
of herself," I replied. "She's thoroughly at
home here, and does as she likes."

"Mr Stewart, I think you're very good-
natured."

"I hope I am," I answered, thinking, had I
been so in the past, it was over, and that in
future I should study the comfort of one person
only, and that one person—Edith Grenville.

"Take me in, please, it is chilly here," she
said presently I did so, inwardly miserable.
I felt that indoors she would dance with somebody else, and that would be almost more than
I could endure. I am to be spared that agony,
however, for in the hall we meet Hawkes *père*,
in a generally hazy state of mind, but conscious
that his carriage horses have been waiting half
an hour.

"Good-night, my boy," he says, shaking hands
for the second time. "I wish I'd seen more of
you to-night, but, somehow, I couldn't come

across you. I say, excellent dry sherry that of yours! I stuck to *it* as I couldn't see *you.*"

I blessed that sherry in my inmost heart, and fetched Edith's wrap.

Somehow, going down the steps to the carriage, I was, in spite of contrary endeavours, beside Georgy.

"Poor old Prince," she whispered, putting her hand upon my arm; "but I'll do all I can for you—come to luncheon to-morrow."

I fancy the lights must have nearly burnt out when I went back to the house, they seemed dimmed so much.

There is a lot in association!

CHAPTER THE FOURTH.

WHEN a man is *really* in love, he is oblivious of all earthly considerations. That sentiment may not be original, but it is true, which is, perhaps, better.

In a general way I was, I sincerely believe, a cool-headed fellow enough. If I heard that any friend was about to marry, I invariably put the question, "Who is the woman?" And if the reply went to show that she was a barmaid, or a penniless parson's daughter, or anything of that sort, though I admired my friend's pluck, I confess to thinking very little indeed of his discretion. But when my own turn came, I don't think I considered for a single moment that I knew nothing of Edith Grenville's birth or parentage. She appeared to possess a discriminating knowledge of "I," and "me," and those fatal traps for the half-educated, and she certainly did not drop her "h's." This much I knew, and it was quite sufficient.

Even at this distance of time, it seems absurd to talk of her age. It might have been five-and-twenty or five-and-thirty; but, whatever it was, I am certain at no period of her life had she ever looked more beautiful.

Hitherto I had evaded successfully woman and all her works; this time I met my destiny, and succumbed without a murmur.

The night following the dance at the Manor was filled with dreams of love, complicated, in a distressing manner, with tree-ferns. The next morning seemed interminable. How fervently I blessed Georgy in my heart for asking me to luncheon! The only shadow was, that 1.30 p.m. seemed much further off than a year hence does now.

I went down to the village school to see how the theatrical preparations were proceeding; inspected them, talked volumes with the parish clerk (a perfect scene-shifter, and born, I am certain, to adorn any stage); did all this, and found it had scarcely occupied forty minutes!

Somebody—wasn't it Beaconsfield?—said that " everything comes to the man who waits," and undoubtedly it does—if he does not die during his probation. I didn't die, and therefore the hour came to me at which I could turn up at Brandon House. I went there, and trembled as I rang the front door bell. For half a second the horrible thought flashed through me that daylight might reveal flaws and imperfections in my goddess which the lamps of last night had been unable to discover. But another sort of disappointment was in store for me. Edith had a headache, and was upstairs and invisible. I don't know how real or how severe her malady may have been, but supposing any parity between it and my heartache at the intelligence, I pity her!

Georgy took me aside for a few moments before luncheon. There was that unusual mingled expression on her face which I had first seen when she looked into the conservatory last night.

"Well, Prince," she said gaily, "so you are really dreadfully 'gone' at last? I had no idea Edith was half so dangerous; but Eva warned you, I remember."

"But *you* must see how lovely she is," I say rashly. (No rasher act in the world than praising one woman's looks to another—certain to make an enemy for life!)

"Oh, she looks well enough *when she's finished,*" Georgy answers—a bit spitefully, I fancy. "But she takes a terribly long time to dress—she's so *artistic,* you know."

Just at this moment we make a move to the dining-room, there to be pestered by Hawkes on the subject of dry sherry. "It's an excellent drink," he says, "for any one suffering with an affection of the heart." I don't think he *meant* to be funny—he was too dense for that.

Mrs Hawkes was a good-natured, silent old lady, with an appearance of having been severely snubbed by her daughters; which, I fear, was indeed the case. Her great *forte* lay in providing for the inner woman. She was the hardest feeder, bar none, I have ever seen. At meals she was entirely silent, filling internal vacancies, that seemed to be as numerous as those in the daily papers for a gentleman with a thousand pounds at command.

The luncheon was soon over. Georgy took me aside directly afterwards.

"I forgot to tell you one thing, Prince," she said; "I've persuaded Edith to stay with us for a fortnight instead of a week. Are you grateful?"

I solemnly declared that my gratitude could not be expressed in mere words.

"But it can in peaches," she said.

I took the hint at once, and promised—I fancy it was a bushel—that night.

"I hope Edith won't drive your part out of your head this evening at the theatricals," Georgy said presently. "But she doesn't care to see the piece two nights running, so she won't be there."

It was a terrible disappointment, but I made

the best of it, and prepared to go, for it was four o'clock. Georgy accompanied me to the door. At the moment we arrived there, one of the Hawkes's servants handed me a telegram sent on for me from the Manor.

"Am passing through town. Will come to you this day week for three days. Wire reply.   HARRY BECKETT."

The dearest friend I had in the world was Harry Beckett. I saved his life, and made his acquaintance at one and the same time, under perilous circumstances, and the shadow of the rock of Gibraltar, where the upsetting of a boat and a chance knock on the head occurring simultaneously, placed him in great danger.

I don't know why I felt a little annoyed at getting his message. I had not the very slightest fear of his rivalry with Edith, for he was, I knew well, a confirmed woman-hater. But somehow I didn't feel quite pleased as I handed the telegram to Georgy. She read it, and made some casual remark, I forget what. "Send those peaches early, so that I can have some before dressing," were her last words at parting.

The walk home to the Manor was not a long one, but on the way I met Primrose, financially anxious as to the probable result of the night's performance.

"Good up to this—the ticket sales," he said cheerfully, "and I believe it will be a fine night—that is most essential. How well everything went last night! I was positively charmed! Surely they can do no better at a real theatre? I have never been inside one —my wife has scruples."

Poor dear old Primrose! He fought the devil and all his works pluckily enough; but Mrs Primrose was a great deal harder to contend with, and, between ourselves, I believe he feared her much more profoundly of the two. He turned back with me, and walked towards the Manor lodge, through the balmy air, with the first golden victims of Nature's annual death fluttering down to earth, and making *that* golden too.

"You think it will go all right?" the vicar asked me, as we parted at my entrance lodge.

"I trust so."

"I really believe it will be a success in a monetary point of view," he said; "two dissenters have, I hear, taken seats," with which consolatory piece of information he left me.

That night I wired "come" to Harry Beckett.

I have only a very hazy recollection of those theatricals. There was a full house from Mr Primrose's point of view, but a very empty one from mine; for Edith Grenville kept to her determination, and did not appear.

There was a great deal of applause, so I imagine people enjoyed it. I confess I did not. In fact, it bored me, and Georgy Hawkes was so needlessly and demonstratively affectionate to me in the last scene, where husband and wife are reconciled, that I was angry with her.

Primrose came "behind" after it was all over, and thanked me warmly; assuring me the proceeds exceeded his highest anticipations, and mentioning that he had observed the two dissenters laughing till they cried.

This latter circumstance seemed to carry more weight with him that it did with me.

CHAPTER THE FIFTH.

BEFORE parting with the Hawkes at the school after the performance, I observed Georgy whisper to her father, and that individual presently came to me, and delivered a warm, but slightly indistinct, invitation to dine at Brandon House the following evening; coupled with an intimation that he had just obtained some dry sherry "of a quality to surprise a man."

I accepted at once, not wholly on account of the dry sherry.

The day I spent in wandering, in a weak and purposeless manner, through the conservatory, and examining the tree-fern. Somehow it seemed interesting to Edith, and priceless on that account.

There is a strange sense of loneliness that

comes to one in love if separated by any chance circumstance from the object of it. I felt this keenly the day after the theatricals at the school.

The Hawkes dined at seven-thirty, and therefore there was no possible excuse for my presenting myself at their house at seven o'clock, but I did it. I take it as not the first breach of etiquette for which Cupid is responsible.

It is a singular fact that domestics possess a keener perception in the matter of love affairs than their masters or mistresses. The parlour-maid (no man-servant at Brandon House), who opened the door upon my arrival, had a peculiar smile upon her face, though she tried hard to hide it. I recognised that smile at once. I had seen it hovering about her face in the early days of my acquantance with the Hawkes; a smile which, I observed, grew gradually grimmer and still more grim as nothing like an engagement between Georgy and myself transpired. It died out altogether, at last, for lack of proper nourishment, I suppose. Now it was springing up again, in all its pristine progress. The parlour-maid ushered me into the drawing-room straight-way.

The Hawkes's drawing-room was a long one, divided in the centre by curtains draped over pillars. There was a fire (for the night had turned chilly) in the grate at the far end of the room, but no other light in that portion of the apartment; at the end by which I entered there was a lamp, but no fire. This latter part, too, was empty; but, sitting in a low chair close to the distant fire, and guarding her face from it with a fan, sat Edith Grenville. She was in a thoughtful attitude, gazing into the dancing flames. The pose was perfect. I was deeper in love, if possible, than ever. As I approached she turned her head (what a lovely face she had !), and welcomed me in the uncertain light.

" They're all very late to-night," she said, smiling, and glancing at the empty room.

" Are there other people, guests, coming ? " I asked. This horrible contingency had not even entered my mind.

"Only Mr and Mrs Primrose, I believe—
you won't mind *them?*"

"I shall be delighted," I said, "for Primrose
will take in Mrs Hawkes, and Mr Hawkes
will take Mrs Primrose, and I shall take—"

"Your great friend Georgy, of course," Edith
broke in mischievously. "I know that's what
you're counting upon."

At this moment the two girls came in, and ac-
corded me an effusive welcome, and half a moment
later the vicar and his wife are announced.

Mrs Primrose is an austere old lady in black
silk, that crackles in a newspapery sort of
way when she walks.

Vicar and wife are introduced to Edith, and
seem to amuse her, to judge by her expression
as she looks at them. Mr Primrose gazes
upon her with evident admiration, and I
hear him say something to his wife in which
the word "perfect" occurs. I also catch
part of his wife's rejoinder, "terribly got
up." These three words form the last resource of a woman asked to admire one of
her own sex. When you hear a woman say

that so-and-so is ' terribly got up," you may conclude so-and-so is as near perfection as possible. Don't forget this : I never knew it unreliable.

Mr and Mrs Hawkes come in presently, apologising for being late. Hawkes says he never allows anybody but himself to meddle with his wine in the matter of decanting. I fancy he had done more than decant it, from his manner of explanation.

Dinner is announced, and Mrs Hawkes (God bless her !) requests me to take in Edith Grenville. Another lamp has been brought, and the whole room is brightly illuminated. Edith takes my arm, smiling, and whispers, "So you're *not* to take Georgy after all ; I'm *so* sorry for you."

An old-fashioned hall, with your host and vicar's wife immediately ahead of you, and your hostess with the vicar behind, at the distance of only two laughing sisters, is not exactly the strategic position, nor are the circumstances those one would of choice select for declaring a wild, undying passion to the fair one who has aroused it; but I swear no man was ever nearer the fatal brink than I was then and there. But I restrained myself, and walked into a very Eden of a dining-room, where the cooking, at least, I am certain, beat that first Eden to nothing at all.

I don't know what happened during soup, but presently I became aware that I was endeavouring to consume a piece of some sort of fish, and that Primrose was talking of churches; maintaining that ours at Brandon was of remarkable antiquity, whilst Hawkes (effect of dry sherry) was disposed to maintain (though he knew nothing about it) that Brandon church was built within the century.

Brandon church had certainly one remarkable feature: an old library, left by some bygone benefactor to his village, full of musty old books, chiefly Latin, of great interest to antiquaries. Apart from this, there were also quaint old brasses in the aisles, and monuments upon the walls, all of which were worth a visit. Edith expressed a desire to see the place.

"Will you come with me to-morrow?" I asked, with diffidence.

She looked at me and smiled.

"I daresay the girls will come too," she said.

It seemed an age before we were all in the drawing-room again. That confounded dry sherry (whoever heard of such a drink for civilised man in the nineteenth century?) had to be reckoned with, and a tedious process it turned out to be.

When we *did* get away from the dining-room, Edith was looking over Georgy's music, and Mrs Primrose looking at Edith in an austere and disapproving manner, as though somehow her beauty was a personal injury, deeply resented.

"Edith will sing to you now," Georgy said, in a friendly way, and I noticed that my idol whispered something to her, in which I fancied I caught the words, "too bad." I heard, too, in Georgy's reply, "soon get over it," or words to that effect. It was Sanscrit to me then; I can understand it perfectly *now*.

Edith did sing. I don't think there ever was

P

such a voice as hers that night. The song was a simple one, "*Auld Robin Gray.*" I can't hear it now without sadness that is very weak and foolish.

I glanced back, during the singing, from where I was turning over the music leaves, and noticed that even Mrs Primrose was sitting as though impressed, and that Hawkes *père* had actually paused in a full and particular account he was giving the vicar of the recent importation of dry sherry.

After the song was over, Georgy (who didn't sing) played something in a way I have often heard described as brilliant, which I understand to imply great noise and muscular exertion. I didn't take much heed of the music, for I was sitting beside Edith in the recess of a curtained window, lost to outside influences.

"You are making a long stay in Beechshire," I hazarded.

"Only a week," she replied—sadly. I thought.

"Georgy told me your visit was to extend to a fortnight."

"Ah, there was some talk of that, but I have decided to go back to town at the end of the week."

She spoke with the slightest possible hesitation.

"What a terribly short visit!" I exclaim, suddenly plunged in the depths of misery.

She glances quickly at me, and there is a look that might be pity in her bright eyes for a moment; but it quickly gives place to the usual sparkling witchery as she answers,—

"A week! a whole week a terribly short visit! Why, a week is an age—long enough for inaugurating a successful revolution—or for losing one's fortune, or—"

I shall never forget her mischievous glance as she left the sentence unfinished.

I was about to finish it for her, and add "one's heart," when that detestable Mrs Primrose, who was always certain to be just where one didn't wish her, made a sudden swoop upon us, and asked me "if I could remember whether the receipts from the theatricals at the school were ten pounds, seventeen and fivepence, or

ten pounds, five and sevenpence?" and, in spite
of all my curt rejoinders, sat perseveringly
close beside us for the remainder of the
evening.

" We shall *start* with you to-morrow, when
you take Edith to see the church," Georgy said,
when I was leaving. "*Start* with you; but
we *may* have to make a charity call on the
way; in which case, no doubt you will prove
quite equal to taking care of her alone."

For the first time in my life, I think, I squeeze
Georgy's hand. I am so grateful to her for
her thoughtfulness.

"Those peaches are all eaten, Prince," she
rejoins.

CHAPTER THE SIXTH.

THE following afternoon was bright and sunny. I called for the Hawkes and their visitor at half-past three. They were all ready, and a start was made at once. The way to the church lay through the little village of Brandon, and the distance was about half a mile.

We had nearly reached the end of the village street when Georgy and Eva, stating they must call on some decrepit villager, and that they would speedily overtake us, turned into one of the cottages, and left Edith and me to go on to the church alone.

I shall never forget that walk!

Out of the village and through a field

already guilded for harvest; with a stillness in the air, and a haze hanging languidly upon distant woodlands and round the square brick tower of the church, in spite of the bright sunshine lighting up the landscape on every side. Lighting up, too, that wonderfully beautiful face of Edith's; the pale, creamy complexion, the perfect figure; truly a fit companion for such a walk, through such a country !

There never was yet a lovely prospect that could not be made *more* lovely by the presence of a lovely woman. Nature and human nature assimilate so well! Ah! it is a great privilege to have the one *right* voice out of all the world with one anywhere !

"Yours is a pretty village — a very pretty village," Edith says, as we stroll slowly along.

"It *is* pretty," I reply feebly ; "but it has never appeared to me so pretty as it does to-day."

She smiles. She knows what I mean, and turns her head away, glancing out over the golden landscape dreamily.

We are at the church before I can venture anything further. The old woman who generally points out things of interest to visitors is laid up, so *I* take the key from her daughter, saying, "I know everything worth seeing."

Alone with Edith, into the hush of the sacred building, with its earthy odour and the sunlight streaming in through the western window, throwing rainbow sheens upon tomb and scutcheon.

We inspect everything closely. The musty old books in the library, the quaint mottoes upon the walls, the heavy velvet - covered chairs. I hand the visitors' book to Edith, and she signs it with a signature that is there now; for I often am weak enough— or strong enough—to go and look at it, even in these after-days.

Then out into the aisles of the church, noting the blue sky portrayed above the communion-table, the brasses at our feet, everything of any interest at all. Thence we wander, by a natural transition, into the vestry Nothing of great interest there; a cracked looking-glass upon the wall, together with a table of affinities; these and another table of oak, an iron box, and a chair or two, constitute the furniture of the place.

Upon the oaken table lies a book. Not a very modern one either. It records the publishing of banns of marriage.

Casually I open this book, Edith standing beside me as I do so. There are numerous entries in the feeble writing of the vicar. I turn a page and come to a leaf where Primrose has evidently got into a muddle of some sort, and "tried back," scratching out the entire entry by diagonal lines drawn through it.

"Look there," Edith says, smiling and pointing to the place, "that couple thought better of it, evidently."

The feeling was strong upon me to seize that opportunity and make an offer of my hand, heart, and fortune there and then, but I didn't. I only laughed feebly.

Now this incident of the erased entry may appear a trivial one to mention, but it had a direct bearing upon this whole story; for it marked a change in Edith's conduct towards me. Till then, I firmly believe, she had only been playing with me; henceforward she was more restrained in her manner, which, at this time, I was totally at a loss to understand.

The Hawkes girls turned up before many minutes—we heard their voices in the church, especially Georgy's. No place was very sacred to her.

"Well, Edith, well, Prince," she said, "have you almost finished 'doing' this old church? You've been more than an hour already!"

I said the inspection *was* over, and we all left the building together.

For some reason Edith seemed determined to walk with Eva, and therefore I was compelled to walk with Georgy

"This friend of yours who is coming down: is he good-looking?" she asked me as we went along. It so happened that on the occasions Beckett had visited me, the Hawkes had been from home, and so he and Georgy had never met.

"I believe he is supposed to be good-looking," I told her. "You can see his photo to-morrow night when you are all coming to dine with me.'

"A photo doesn't tell much, it's no criterion as to his 'style' or his money—the latter being a most important item with me," she said, laughing.

"Do you intend *marrying* Harry Beckett, Georgy?" I asked.

"I tell you candidly I intend marrying *some one* before very long. I'm utterly tired of home, father, and his dry sherry—it's disgusting!"

Parental veneration, I fear, was dying fast, even in those days.

"Beckett has, I believe, about two thousand a year, a roving disposition, and, I am afraid, very little belief in women."

"Just the man!" Georgy exclaimed delightedly. "Just the man, I shall go for him."

In my inmost heart I did not greatly tremble for my friend. I had a very strong suspicion that Miss Georgy had "gone" for me to the greatest extent in her power, and *I* had survived it free. Surely Beckett, the professed woman-hater, could do the same.

Having satisfied Georgy as well as I could upon all points concerning my friend wherein she appeared interested, I tried, as delicately as I was able, to discover something of the past of Edith Grenville.

It did not appear that the Hawkes knew very much about her. They made her acquaintance whilst staying in the same hotel in Switzerland some years ago, and liked her ; and that was all they knew. So Georgy said, but I have the very gravest doubts whether *she*, at least, did not know something more, and purposely withhold it from me.

It had been arranged that the Hawkes should dine at the Manor the following evening, as I have said, and I reminded the girls of it at parting.

" Oh, we sha'n't forget," Georgy replied. " Very likely I shall be over during the day fishing your lake. That lake *must* be re-stocked, Prince."

I made some reply—I forget the words, for I was saying *adieu* to Edith. " And you won't have a headache, and you *will* come to-morrow night ? "

" Perhaps—I suppose so," but there was a smile upon her lips that said more than those simple words.

CHAPTER THE SEVENTH.

EDITH *did* come the following evening with the Hawkes. I was in the dining-room waiting to receive them sooner than either of the other two making up the Manor home circle. Dear old Wade and my aunt followed very quickly, however, and we had a little conversation on the goodness of mankind and womankind in general, before the Hawkes were announced. I recollect that the dinner seemed interminable, chiefly, I suspect, from the fact that I had to take in Mrs Hawkes, and to listen attentively to what she said in those rare moments wherein she paused in her eating.

When the dinner was over, and we were in the drawing-room, or at least when the ladies and myself were in the drawing-room (for I left Wade and Hawkes to discuss the sherry), Georgy came up to me with that mingled expression in her face which I had only recently seen there, and said,—

"Prince, here's a disappointment for you; Edith is obliged to go back to London to-morrow."

"To-morrow!" I exclaimed; "to-morrow!"

"Yes," Edith said softly, joining us. "I am obliged to go back to London to-morrow—the Fates you know," smiling, "the Fates must be obeyed."

"The Fates" have always appeared to me to exist simply for the purpose of separating those who wish to remain together, or, if they have other mission, it lies in the keeping of those people together who would give anything on earth to be apart.

Presently Edith and I strolled out beneath the heavy curtains into the conservatory. Lighted by the many-coloured lanterns; with the sparkling fountain and the odorous blossoms, it was a fairyland to me.

I had all sorts of thoughts passing through my mind, even to verses suggesting the wisdom of putting it

"   To the touch, to win or lose it all."

But if a man *does* fear his fate too much—how then? and that was my exact position. I had only known Edith a few days, though it *seemed* years, and then, too, sometimes I fancied she was laughing at me and my devotion. Altogether, I dared not "put it to the touch," so I made some half-hearted remark as to the suddenness of her departure instead.

Before we had been ten minutes in the conservatory, Eva, who never by any possibility fancied she *could* be in the way, joined us, and that was the end of everything.

For the residue of the evening, we had to endure Georgy's muscular brilliance at the piano.

I begged so hard for *one* song from Edith, before they all went away, that she was obliged to consent. Sitting down at the piano—without music—she sang "*Robin Adair*" (that dear old song!) as I have never heard it sung since.

In no time at all, it seemed to me, the Hawkes's carriage was announced.

"I'm good for walking home—what do you say, Edith? It's not far — what do you say, Eva? Prince will walk with us, I'm certain," said Georgy, as we stood on the front steps.

It was certainly a fine night. The moonlight upon the landscape made it a silver fairy-land — but then, a man's evening dress is not exactly what one would select for pedestrian excursions down dusty roads.

However, the girls were all provided with thick wraps, and, above all, Edith said she should prefer walking, and so it was settled —Mr and Mrs Hawkes going home in the brougham together.

What a walk that was! A walk right into Paradise with Edith Grenville! I don't think it ever occurred to me that a woman so beautiful had probably hundreds of knights sworn to allegiance; amongst whom, perhaps, might be one more admirable and more admired than myself. But then I was in Paradise, and Paradise would not be worth that name if we. were disturbed by tormenting common-sense therein. I only knew that it was Edith's hand resting upon my arm; that it was Edith's voice sounding in my ears; only this I knew—and it was enough.

All too soon the sunshine of this world fades away; all too soon the lengthening shadows steal out from their lurking places, and fall across our path; all too soon—or all too late—before we have fully tasted, or not till we have lived bitterly to repent tasting at all—the cup is dashed from our lips, and broken beyond all repairing!

The half mile dividing the Manor from the Hawkes' house seemed but a hundred yards that night.

"You will be coming down here again?" I pleaded, standing, with Edith's hand in mine, on the white, dusty road, where the branching oaks threw an inky shadow.

Q

"Ask your friends *that;* I can't invite my-self," she laughed.

"Look here, Prince ; it's very shabby of you to leave us at the end of the avenue; come as far as the front door," Georgy said at that moment.

Anything in the world to prolong the time with Edith! So I went on up the carriage-drive, and said good-bye at the hall door.

I turn and look back, when I have gone some little way homeward down the carriage-way. The girls are all out on the steps look-ing after me. There is a grand old cedar near the house, and its shadow falls upon the group. Still I can see both the Hawkes' girls indis-tinctly, but the darkness falls so thick upon Edith, that I cannot distinguish her from the sombre masses of ivy covering the house. In the shadow of those branching cedar arms she is blotted out. So ever, always shadows lying between us and what is dearest in our sight !

CHAPTER THE EIGHTH.

"BECKETT, old fellow, how are you?"

"Delighted to see you again, and well."

Both greetings being spoken simultaneously, and accompanied by a hearty handshake, on the afternoon of my friend's arrival.

"How cosy you look here, Stewart."

It was true. A wood fire blazed up the capacious chimney; my dog Solomon was enjoying the genial heat, stretched upon the hearth-rug; two lamps (I hate a dim light) made the room bright and cheerful; a box of cigars, open, on a side table by my easy-chair, and a certain perfume in the air, told that the greatest of all imported blessings was not forbidden there. It *was* a cheerful picture, no doubt.

"Can I give you anything?" I asked, looking approvingly at the manly form of my friend. He was seeming perhaps a bit older than when I saw him last; but that is the everyday lot of poor humanity The confidence trick of Time, who says, "Trust your youth with me for a few years, for it I will give you knowledge," and we do so, and Mr Time walks off with those days of our innocence for ever.

" Can I give you anything ? "

" Nothing, thanks, but a cigar."

So we two old chums sit one each side the fire, for it is chilly towards seven p.m., and smoke in silence for some time.

" What have *you* been doing ? " I ask presently.

" Travelling—my old amusement. Through Palestine lately."

" Interesting ? "

" Yes. All new places are interesting to me. I can do anything save stay quietly in England. My nature rebels against your English respectability and taxes."

" But you *could* remain steadily in England once ? You told me when I first met you at

Gibraltar that you had only just commenced travelling."

A shadow fell across his face. I had long suspected there was a dark spot in his life, that he would not confide—even to me. I fancied he had lost money; a great deal.

" Manners change, and so do men," he answered quietly.

Before I can say more the dressing-bell rings and we are obliged to part.

The dinner passes off pleasantly enough. Wade and my aunt are as agreeable as possible, and we have all good appetites, thank God!

Beckett and I sit up till past midnight, talking of old faces and mutual friends.

"You're looking *well*, old fellow!" he says, suddenly breaking off in the middle of a sentence. " *Well*—but *changed* somehow. What have you been up to?"

I think guiltily of Edith, and make some vague reply.

"Is it falling in love with your fair friends, the Hawkes—one or both?"

He has often heard of them, though he has never seen them.

"That's what *you're* going to do—fall in love with Georgy (alias Georgina) at first sight. She's quite ready—eager—bent on marrying you, in fact."

"Obliging of her, considering she has never seen me; but somehow I don't think she'll succeed."

"Are you *never* going to succumb to feminine seductions ? "

" Never ! "

There is no mistaking the resolution of his tone.

" But Georgy is very nice; plays brilliantly, and all that. Dear papa is perhaps a bit too fond of dry sherry—but you won't marry the whole family ? "

"Nor any one of them," he replies very quietly, and so the subject drops.

For a long time after leaving him at his bedroom door, I lay awake, thinking what a fine character his was, how resolute, how strong, and wishing I was only half as resolute or half as strong.

CHAPTER THE NINTH.

THE following day Georgy and her sister, the latter being always used by her as a sort of "stalking horse," when in pursuit of male game, called upon us early and were introduced to Beckett.

I could hardly help laughing at the determined way in which Georgy "went for him." I was obliged to promise we would both dine with the Hawkes that night.

"How do you like her?" I asked later in the day, when an opportunity presented itself for the question.

"Rather amusing; no beauty; feel completely safe," was his reply.

That night, at the Hawkes' dinner-table, there was a marked change in the behaviour of dear papa. Whether his youngest daughter had told him that Beckett was the man she meant to marry, or whether he himself was sharp enough to think him a very suitable man, I don't know; but it is certain that Hawkes was that night more abstemious in the matter of dry sherry, and less generally cloudy and confused in mind, than I had ever seen him.

There was a high-handed way with Georgy towards Beckett that was most amusing, even to a man in my state of romantic attachment to an absent fair one.

"Come in here with me, Mr Beckett," she said after dinner, and leading the way into a smaller room off the drawing-room. "I've a painting I want to show you."

Beckett followed with the air of a martyr.

That painting took such a long time to exhibit, that it was nearly time for us to be going before they emerged again.

Smoking together alone that night I repeated my question.

"How do you like her?"

"Very amusing; not altogether ugly; by no means bad form."

Then, for the first time, I began to tremble for Beckett.

His sorrow, whatever its nature, was of the long ago. This girl Georgy, a clever girl, too, was bringing all her powers to bear for his subjugation. I trembled for him, because I had so often heard her say how tired she was of her home; how ready she was to leave it with the first man offering, who could provide her with a more comfortable one. Here *was* the man, and she did not mean to let him escape. I went to bed with a most uncomfortable fear, added to my trouble and uncertainty about Edith.

I was heartily glad when the three days of Beckett's visit passed, and he left me. Georgy certainly made the best use of her time. But when he left, he left free and unhampered by any engagement. I know this, for I asked him candidly, for my own peace of mind.

"Perfectly free; I have not spoken a word to her," he answered.

CHAPTER THE TENTH.

AFTER Beckett left I noticed a change in Georgy. I cannot define it otherwise than as a change. It made me ruminative, and the outcome of this state was, I came to the conclusion Georgy —Georgy the practical—Georgy the quick and practical—was in love.

I don't know *how* I came to this decision; but it forced itself upon me, and would not be shaken off.

I came upon her one day, some weeks after Beckett's departure, fishing my lake.

"Good sport?" I asked, sitting down beside her, and taking the rod out of her hands. "Why Georgy, you've actually no *bait* on the hook!"

For the first time, I think, I saw something like a blush on her face as she replied,—

"I do believe I've forgotten all about the bait. But I didn't want them to bite to-day; fishing seems rather cruel, doesn't it?"

Those words told me my suspicions were correct: she *was* in love. I had noticed lately, too, that she was altogether more *womanish*, and what shall I say?—toned down.

"'Then we'll talk," I said, thinking this a good occasion to hear something about Edith. "Have you heard from Miss Grenville lately, Georgy?"

"We don't correspond every day, Prince. I've told you that already; but I *did* hear from her this morning, as it happens. She is very well and busy."

"Busy?" I asked feebly Surely she could have no occupation. I could as soon fancy Juno mending socks.

"Yes, busy. You know she paints, don't you? That's why she's so fond of flowers. She paints. Very well, too. A great man told her she only required a stimulus—say a misfortune of some sort—to put her in the front rank."

"She never told *me* all this," I said doubtingly.

'You don't suppose she told you *everything*, do you?" queried Georgy.

I confessed I did not quite expect such confidence.

"She's mad about flowers; paints hardly anything else. Why don't you send her some?"

"Would she be—"

"Delighted? Yes, I'm sure *she* would—try her."

I inwardly resolved to do so, forthwith.

"How do you like my friend?" I asked, with as much disconcerting suddenness as I could.

For the second time that day Georgy blushed.

"He's capital," she answered. "Why have we never met before? We might have met before—"

"Before *what*?" I ask.

"Do you know his history?" (taking no notice of my question).

"Only in rough outline—scarcely anything; he's not communicative about himself."

"No; he's not; you're quite right; but *I* can read between the lines."

"Have you read *him*?" (wondering what the feminine power of instinct had told her).

"Yes; like a book."

"Worth the perusal?"

"Quite."

"And what was the story about?"

"About—a love disappointment."

"The deuce it was!" I exclaimed, rather pleased at her mistake. "*I* think it was money."

"But he has got over it. Not *quite*, but *nearly*; he's *getting* over it," she added, taking no notice of my mundane suggestion.

"Georgy, you're a witch."

"Prince, you're a duffer."

"Complimentary, but, I believe, true."

"Then he *has* had some love-affair?" Georgy said. She never let a subject drop till she had done with it.

"I don't really know. I always thought it a money affair—but he not has told me himself."

"Do you think a man's any the *worse* for having had one *real* affair?" Georgy asked, after a longish pause, with her eyes fixed upon the rising fish that she did not see.

"That, I think, depends—"

"On *what?*" she asked, quite sharply. There was no doubt but that she was hard hit.

"Depends upon the strength of the attack, and the result of it. If the furnace is only moderately heated the metal may come out malleable. But a man tried by too fierce a fire, may come out with a cinder in place of a heart."

"But a cinder of *good coal* may be worth more than coal itself of an inferior quality."

"*I* always burn Wallsend," said a voice quite close at hand, making us both start. It was only old Primrose, who had approached unheard upon the grass.

"So do we, I believe," Georgy said, not a bit disconcerted by this sudden arrival on the scene.

"I came to consult you about the new Highway Rate," Primrose went on, addressing me, "and I caught sight of you here as I crossed the park. But, I must confess, with such romantic surroundings, I didn't expect to hear you discussing house coal!"

"It was merely hyperbole — metaphor — fable — trope — or whatever the word is," Georgy said. "We were talking of the sort of person one ought to marry; what is your opinion, Mr Primrose?"

To a man who did not know us both, and the friendly relations in which we stood, this remark might have led to the supposition that his arrival had been most inopportune. Fortunately the Vicar knew us both too well for this, and therefore set his mind to answer Georgy's question, first sitting down upon a rustic seat close by, in a position for meditation.

"The sort of person one ought to marry?" he repeated slowly, to get it firmly fixed in his mind. "That is a tremendously difficult problem! How to select the *right* person to

sit opposite one at breakfast every morning
say, out of all the world? I say 'at breakfast,' for that is the principle I go upon with
regard to matrimony, take care of the breakfast, and the dinner will take care of itself!
Undoubtedly, it is a great blessing and privilege
to be allowed the right face opposite one at
breakfast."

Poor old Primrose spoke with the melancholy
tone of a man conscious of having, personally,
the *wrong* face opposite him at the early meal,
and of having had it, and of being compelled to
look at it, daily, till he had grown very weary
of it!

Georgy *looks* this at me, and smiles. I recollect what I heard Mrs Primrose say of Edith,
and smile too grimly.

"But what is the *outcome* of your theories?"
I asked. Primrose belonged to a large class:
that whose members have a vast number of
theories, but can never deduce any practice
worth mentioning from them. A class who
may be called "great thinkers," being totally
distinct from "great doers."

"The outcome is, that I advise great caution in the selection of a partner for life," the Vicar said, and so fully justified my estimate of him, for I take it a man with no theories at all on the subject would arrive at the same conclusion.

"Do you think a ten-penny Rate?" the Vicar began, anxious to get his work in hand done: but Georgy was not going to let the subject drop thus.

"What sort of person would you advise me to marry, then?" she asked, regardless of his feeble question.

"I think," he replied, "we should put aside all feelings of romance, and look upon the person to whom we feel drawn (if I may use that term) in the light of a brother or sister; look upon them thus, and ask ourselves, firmly and honestly, can I be content to live with so and so all my life? For, depend upon it, if the reply of that question be 'no,' a little romance thrown in will never make the eternal companionship bearable."

It was one of the most sensible remarks,

R

without qualification, I ever heard Primrose make.

"Then you don't believe in romance," Georgy asked.

"Romance?" replied the Vicar, "is sometimes apt to wear off."

He spoke so sadly, that I am certain it had all long ago worn off in his own case.

"I think I must be going," Georgy said, rising; "it's very near luncheon time," and so she left us.

I know *why* she went. It was the realistic turn our conversation had taken. It is terribly hard for Youth to be told, "all your love and devotion, that now seems adamant, will prove only wax in the sunshine of reality some day, after all: the fatal word 'Dead' be written against the fairest flower in the heart's garden!"

Mr Primrose stayed luncheon with me, and we settled the Highway Rate over a cigar afterwards.

"I can't imagine," said Wade, who with myself accompanied the Vicar to the door later, "I can't imagine why Cupid is always depicted with *wings*," and he stopped before a statuette to point out what he meant.

As long as I live I shall never forget the mingled look of drollery and sadness upon poor old Primrose's face as he replied,—

"Because he *has* been known to fly, I should imagine."

CHAPTER THE ELEVENTH.

"Fain would I climb, but I fear to fall.
If thy heart fail thee, climb not at all."

EXACTLY like a woman, wasn't it? Elizabeth
was a true woman in spite of all detractors.
No one, reading the second (her) line of the fore-
going diamond-cut couplet, could doubt it.

Such a vague reply to a protestation of love
and ambition! The "if" was the difficulty.
After reading the Queen's reply it must almost have been conquered; but not *quite*, or
English history, might have read differently to-
day. All this is put in my thoughts by a
letter, faded and old like myself, that is lying
upon the table where I write.

It is a memorable letter, in a sense too,

for it is the only one I ever received from
Edith Granville.

I took Georgy's hint about the flowers, and
obtaining the address, forwarded such a basket
of blossom as, I believe, was never beaten by
Covent Garden.

With the basket a letter of explanation, too,
of course; I forget the words, but I know
it expressed a fervent hope that Brandon
would be gladdened by Edith's early presence
there. It was in reply to this note I received
these few lines :—

"DEAR MR STEWART,—I am sure I can never
thank you sufficiently for the beautiful flowers!
They are now placed all about my room, so that
which ever way I look, I am face to face with
them. I am going to paint some of them. The
pleasure of so doing will be very great to me.
Again thanking you.—Believe me, sincerely yours,
                    "EDITH GRENVILLE."

"Nothing in it," I am certain every reader
will say at once. But the top-sparkle

moments of our lives are very tame, and indescribable on paper.

It was soon after receiving this letter that something very like a happy thought flashed upon me.

Beckett was still in England. Now, would it not be quite possible to make an exchange of prisoners with Georgy somehow in this way,—

"You have Edith down again, and after she is gone, I will get Beckett to the Manor again." Such, I imagined, a most satisfactory arrangement, and I determined to set about it at once.

That very morning I strolled down to the lake, for it was fine, and I rightly calculated upon finding Georgy fishing there.

Approaching the water I found I was not wrong. Georgy *was* there, but not quite in her usual place, for instead of being on the grass, she was seated upon the bench Primrose used the other day, and—reading.

I don't think I ever saw her with a book in her hand before; but all the metamorphoses of Ovid are nothing to compare with those of Cupid!

"Ah! Prince," she said, rising and putting down the book (which to my utter surprise I saw was Moore's Poems), "ah, Prince, I wanted to see you, badly; I've wonderful news for you."

"Good news, I hope," I said, sitting down on the beach beside her.

"The best in the world, I fancy," she laughed. "Edith writes to say that if we can have her on Saturday—"

"*Next* Saturday?" I asked eagerly, for the the day I write of was a Thursday.

"Next Saturday, and she'll stay over Sunday, and return to town on Tuesday. *Is* that good news?"

"Well, I'm delighted to hear it; so I suppose it is," I answered.

Her book was lying open at "Love's Young Dream."

"I didn't know you went in for poetry," I said, taking up the volume. "Do you like Moore?"

"I don't like *that*," she answered, indicating the poem I have mentioned ; "and I don't believe it, do *you?*"

"The whole of it? I didn't know there was anything to believe," I answered, perplexed.

"Look at the two last lines :—

> "'Twas a light that ne'er can shine again
> On life's dull stream."

"Do you believe *that?* Because I don't; I think it bosh."

Somehow Georgy and her phraseology seemed unfitted for discussing poetry. Look at it which way you will, the word "bosh," though oriental and forcible, is jarring applied to poetry.

"We are getting to the same ground we beat over here with Primrose," I said quietly. "You have become so changed and romantic, Georgy, that I begin to feel quite a stranger to you. I shall have to call you 'Miss Hawkes' soon, if this sort of thing continues."

"Do you know," Georgy said, smiling rather a sad smile, "do you know that Edith is coming, because someone *asked* her to do so—

begged her to do so — in point of fact, my self ? "

"It was very kind and considerate of you. What can I do by way of return ? "

"I wonder whether your wandering friend is still in England ? " she asked dreamily. So she had had a "happy thought" too!

"Do you know, Prince," she went on, "I feel *spiteful*. That's why I've asked Edith here. Strange—isn't it ?—but perfectly true."

There was that unwonted expression in her face as she spoke.

"I don't mind how often you feel spiteful, if you invite Edith Grenville here each time," I replied, laughing.

"It's the most cruel thing I can do for you — I'm half inclined — but no, I've made a promise, and I mustn't break it."

"I shouldn't wonder if I have a spiteful fit, and invite Beckett before very long," I answered.

"Ah! *that's* different. Poor old Prince ! "

I didn't understand it in the least then — I do now, perfectly.

CHAPTER THE TWELFTH.

"AND you really liked the flowers?"

"And I really liked the flowers — immensely."

Edith and I were talking in the Manor drawing-room the Monday evening of her visit. The Hawkes had been dining with me, and of course Edith too. And at the moment, thank God! Georgy was dashing off something "brilliant" at the piano, and it had the extra advantage of being *long*.

"They all came out of my houses; I'm glad you liked them."

"All out of your own houses? What a beautiful place this is! Has the house been "restored?" If so, it was done very judiciously."

"I had a little done to it; I will show you a photo of the place before the restoration."

The Manor drawing-room is a long one, and the photo book is at the far end of it; when I return, book in hand, Edith has gone through the curtains into the conservatory, and is sitting by the familiar tree - fern, amid the varied blooms — a thousand times prettier than the fairest of them.

I sit down by her on the couch; for some reason I don't open the album. I take Edith's hand instead, and say,—

"This place is never really pretty to me when you are not here—would it be very hard for you to stay always?"

Edith does not withdraw her hand, but she is strangely silent, looking down. In the hush the plash of the fountain - drops, as they fall, might be Cupid weeping.

Suddenly she turns her face towards me with the saddest expression upon it human face ever wore.

"Oh, Mr Stewart!" she exclaims, in a broken voice. "I am so dreadfully sorry — I ought

never to have come here a second time — and
yet — and yet—" Her voice falters, and she
stops.

"What *does* all this mean: that you hate
me?" I ask bitterly, for her manner tells me
there is no hope. I even let go her hand; but
she gently places it in mine again, as she says,—

"It means that I am a hypocrite, sailing under
false colours, and now justly punished. It means
that you must never see me; never think of
me after to-night: for my sake as well as yours,
that you must forget me utterly."

"But I am completely lost. What bar can
there be between us?"

"A bar that can never be removed save by
death."

Then I understood her: she was married.

"I was foolish enough to adopt my maiden
name when—when we separated, I never dreamed
of this result, never!"

"But are both our lives to be blighted beyond
hope? is there no way—"

"There is *no* way; *no* hope; nothing left
for us but to endure."

And Edith, weeping very bitterly all the while, lays her head for an instant upon my shoulder.

I scarcely realised it all even then. I only knew that the world was nothing to me henceforth; that all my future days were days of darkness.

And, through all, that most brilliant piece Georgy was playing, went on—on—on—like fate; or, as the funeral music at the burial of my happiness, I thought, I heard this something played the other day, and felt dizzy and miserable, after all these years.

"Can you ever forgive me?" Edith asked, looking up at me sadly.

And I only whispered a reply, and kissed her.

What a different world it seemed to me, when we joined the others again! what a different world it *has* been ever since!

CHAPTER THE THIRTEENTH.

IN spite of my sorrow I had to keep my word to Georgy, and ask Beckett to the Manor. Contrary to my expectation, he accepted.

I was in the library, as on the former occasion of his former visit, when he arrived.

"Stewart, my boy, how bad you're looking!" those were his first words of greeting.

"I'm not quite the thing, but it's nothing serious; I'm glad you've come. I didn't quite expect you, to tell the truth."

I fancied he looked rather guilty as he spoke, and there was something of the sort in his voice as he replied,—

"You know I love this old place, and am always glad to come here."

"I'm sure Georgy will be delighted to see you."

A momentary flush of pleasure came and went on his sunburnt face.

"I believe you're chaffing," he said. But, as though he hoped I were not, I thought.

"Not in the least; it's absolute fact."

But we had no long time for private discussion then; for Wade and my aunt came into the room almost simulutaneously, and the conversation became general.

It is a strange fact that, upon every subject broached at the Manor, these two, Wade and my aunt, agreed to a nicety If the romance of love is possible after seventy, those two experienced it to the full. But then they weren't married!

The days of Beckett's visit went by very quickly, but I saw little of him.

He passed his time almost exclusively with Georgy, fishing, or pretending to fish, or taking long walks with her about the surrounding country.

What little I *did* see of him—whether alone

or with Georgy—convinced me that the fatal spell of propinquity was working surely, as it ever does; that they were in fact, though not in name, lovers.

It was rather a relief just at that time to be left alone with my own sorrow, to conquer it if I could.

Sometimes, without the least idea of how much she knew, I fancied there was a smile of something very like triumph on Georgy's face when she saw the sadness of mine. When I recalled what she said about spite in having Edith at Brandon House, I was sure of it. There was something so essentially *womanish* about introducing to the man *she* could not subdue, a beauty who should conquer him, and yet could, by no possibility, be his.

Beckett and I were sitting smoking together one night towards the end of his visit. I was morally certain he had something on his mind. I could see it in his abstraction, and absent replies to my remarks.

"Old fellow," he began suddenly, "old fellow— I'm in a devil of a mess."

"I'm awfully sorry to hear it," I answered. "Is it money? If it's money—"

"I know what you're going to offer, it's like your liberality," he broke in, "but it's *not* money. It's something far worse—I'm in love."

"I've guessed that these five days — with Georgy?"

"Yes."

"Well—there's nothing very terrible about that. It's only a case of ask and ye shall receive."

"Oh, Stewart! if you only knew *all!*"

He spoke in a tone of such utter misery, that I looked at him aghast.

"I've never told you—I never talk of it—" he went on; "but you recollect my saying once that my life was a shadowed life?"

"Perfectly."

"That shadow is a woman's shadow."

I don't know how, or why, but suddenly a horrible, but intangible, dread was upon me, and I only said yes, very feebly.

"It's painful to speak about it—doubly painful *now*."

"Then *don't* speak of it, old fellow."

S

"I *must* speak, before it goes further. Some-one must tell her—I *cannot.*"

I dimly perceived that the painful duty would fall upon me.

"Never mind *when*," he went on, after an evident effort to summon up resolution for the task. Never mind *where*—before I met you—I fell in love; for the first time in my life. I thought her an angel—so she would have been, perhaps, to any other man than myself. My love had a terrible awakening. When it was too late, we discovered that we were totally unsuited to each other; that there were differ-ences between us that made it impossible we could struggle on in company. Under our system of civilisation one can never find this out *before* marriage."

He paused, and I could see by his troubled look that he was back again in that stormy past. The indefinable feeling of dread was upon me, more strongly than before; I feared his next words intensely, but I felt them, and knew positively what they were, long, long before he spoke them.

"My wife still lives. With any other man

she would be happy; could probably make him so—she can only make *me* miserable."

Still in a nightmare, I asked his wife's maiden name; knowing it with a horrible certainty all the time.

"Edith Grenville."

He had no idea how his words pained me— he never will know. He was silent, whilst I mused on the strangeness of it all. The man whose life I had saved was Ediths husband. The woman whom Georgy had introduced to me from motives of revenge was the wife of the man Georgy herself now wished to marry. What a world of cross purposes! What a heap of trouble could have been averted had Georgy only known more than that Edith was married; known who Edith's husband was!"

"Stewart, old fellow! *you* will tell Georgy, for I cannot; I shall leave early to-morrow morning, probably for ever."

For a moment conflicting emotions choked my speech, then I said,—

"Yes,   I will tell her."

CHAPTER THE LAST.

WHATEVER other faults (no doubt many) may be justly laid at my door, vindictiveness is not among them.

As I stood the following morning on the railway station, bidding farewell to Beckett, and thought of the task I had undertaken with respect to Georgy, I was only sorry for her. Though her spite had been so bitter, I could be only sorry for her as I stood there that sunny morning.

"Good-bye, old fellow," he said, as the train steamed into the station. "If ever I come here, or see you again, I will thank you as I ought for all your goodness to me: at this moment I cannot."

It was true. I could see he had a hard mutter to keep back his emotion as he spoke.

"Good-bye, we shall meet again, never fear," I said, with a last hand-shake. And I think so still, but it will be beyond the dark grave —the great river—in the streets of gold.

He will never return to England.

I walked back to the Manor, and half-way across the park met Georgy going towards the lake.

"Where is Mr Beckett?" she asked. "I expected to see him before this."

"I doubt if you will ever see him again," I answered. "He has left; he starts to-morrow for the East."

"Queer, isn't it? she asked demurely.

"Not at all, Georgy, he was fast falling in love with you."

"Well?"

"A married man is not supposed to fall in love."

"Married!" she exclaimed, with a slight start.

"Yes, and you know his wife."

"*I* do? Surely not—"

"Yes, Georgy, Edith is his wife."

There was silence for a minute or more, and then she said the strangest thing in the world.

"Never mind, Prince, *it's a bit of a sell*, but don't trouble—I sha'n't—we're quits."

I am inclined to think "heart" amongst women a rare exception.

"It's a bit of a sell," she repeated, presently, and then pressed me as to the re-stocking of the lake.

From that moment, I believe, she dismissed the subject of Beckett utterly out of her mind. Within six months she was engaged to a gentleman of great wealth (and age), who, to her father's unspeakable delight, was connected with dry sherry—wholesale.

For two years I saw nothing of Edith, when chance gave me a last glance at her. I was at a reception given by the wife of a great artist in London. Towards midnight, the rooms being very hot and very crowded, I managed to edge my way through a press

of people (each one of whom had done something in the world, and will certainly have
an obituary notice of at least an inch and a
half in the *Times* when all other times are
over for them), and so got out on to the stairs
and down them.

There was a recessed window on those stairs
decked with palms and other greenery. Seated
on a lounge in this recess, with a suspended
lamp above her, was Edith, glancing out into
the wet winter street beneath. The expression
of her face was sadder, but more beautiful, than
when I knew her.

In the hall I encountered a General of Division
whom I knew; he was happy and hungry,
and talking of dropping in at the club for
supper.

"General," I said, taking him aside, "you
know everyone; who is the woman in the
recess?"

I wanted to hear what the world said of
her.

"What! don't you know her? Most extra-
ordinary woman! A Mrs Beckett. Made a

great (and first) hit in the Academy this year with an oriental picture, containing a tree-fern you could lean up against, Stewart —positively *lean* up against; it's said to be the most remarkable thing in that line extant. Took the judges and all London by storm. She's an immense celebrity, as great, in her way as you."

Declining, kindly but friendly, the General's hospitable offer of a "quiet devil at the club," I saw the warrior safely into his brougham and returned for my hat, and one last glance at Edith.

She still sat there, as when I first saw her. And she was famous! The one thing the great man said her work wanted had come to her, and she was famous!

I, too, in the sorrow of that unforgetable past, became a devotee of art, though not with the brush. I, too, have made a name in the world, and other changes have come to my home-life, which it is needless to mention here. But I fancy she and I would gladly —even now—yield all we have achieved since those old days at Brandon, if it were wise or well for us to meet once more. I think her studio is as blankly empty as I know my study is. I think so because, from what I hear—from what her face told me that last time I saw it—I gather that time has brought as little forgetfulness to her heart as to mine; that with her, as with me, memory retains a central figure which will not fade away.

THE END.

COLSTON AND COMPANY, PRINTERS, EDINBURGH.

NOVELS.

Price 2s. In Picture Boards.

AN AUSTRALIAN HEROINE. By Mrs Campbell Praed.

ANTONY GRACE. By G. Manville Fenn.

AS IN A LOOKING GLASS. By F. C. Philips.

BIRD OF PASSAGE, A. By B. M. Croker.

CANON LUCIFER. By J. D. Delille.

CHEQUERS, THE. By James Runciman.

COQUETTE'S CONQUEST, A. By 'Basil.'

DEAN AND HIS DAUGHTER, THE. By F. C. Philips.

DINGY HOUSE AT KENSINGTON, THE.

DOUBLE CUNNING. By G. Manville Fenn.

DUKE'S SWEETHEART, THE. By R. Dowling.

EARLY FROST, AN. By C. R. James.

FLOWER OF DOOM, THE. By M. Betham-Edwards.

FOLLY MORRISON. By Frank Barrett.

GREAT PORTER SQUARE. By B. L. Farjeon.

GRETCHEN. By 'Rita.'

GRIF By B. L. Farjeon.

HANDSOME JACK. By James Greenwood.

HEAD STATION, THE. By Mrs Campbell Praed.

HER TWO MILLIONS. By William Westall.

HONEST DAVIE. By Frank Barrett.

HOUSE OF WHITE SHADOWS, THE. By B. L. Farjeon.

HUSBAND AND WIFE. By Marie Connor.

IN ONE TOWN. By Edmund Downey

IN A SILVER SEA. By B. L. Farjeon.

IN THE FLOWER OF HER YOUTH. By Mabel Collins.

JACK AND THREE JILLS. By F. C. Philips.

LADYE NANCYE, THE. By 'RITA.'

LIFE'S MISTAKE, A. By MRS H. LOVETT CAMERON.

LOUISA. By K. S. MACQUOID.

LUCKY YOUNG WOMAN, A. By F. C. PHILIPS.

MAIDEN ALL FORLORN, A. By the Author of 'Molly Bawn.'

MARVEL. By the Author of 'Molly Bawn.'

MASTER OF THE CEREMONIES, THE. By G. M. FENN.

MENTAL STRUGGLE, A. By the Author of 'Molly Bawn.'

MISER FAREBROTHER. By B. L. FARJEON.

MODERN CIRCE, A. By the Author of 'Molly Bawn.'

MODERN MAGICIAN, A. By FITZGERALD MOLLOY.

NUN'S CURSE, THE. By MRS RIDDELL.

OLD FACTORY, THE. By WILLIAM WESTALL.

ONE MAID'S MISCHIEF. By G. M. FENN.

PRETTIEST WOMAN IN WARSAW, THE. By MABEL COLLINS.

PRETTY MISS NEVILLE. By B. M. CROKER.

PRINCE OF THE BLOOD, A. By JAMES PAYN.

PROPER PRIDE. By B. M. CROKER.

RALPH NORBRECK'S TRUST. By WILLIAM WESTALL.

RED RYVINGTON. By WILLIAM WESTALL.

REIGNING FAVOURITE, A. By ANNIE THOMAS.

SACRED NUGGET, THE. By B. L. FARJEON.

SCHEHERAZADE. By the Author of 'The House on the Marsh.'

SOCIAL VICISSITUDES. By F. C. PHILIPS.

TEMPEST DRIVEN. By RICHARD DOWLING.

TERRIBLE LEGACY, A. By G. W. APPLETON.

THAT VILLAIN ROMEO. By J. FITZGERALD MOLLOY.

THIS MAN'S WIFE. By G. M. FENN.

THROUGH GREEN GLASSES. By F. M. ALLEN.

TRAGEDY OF FEATHERSTONE, THE. By B. L. FARJEON.

UNDER ST PAUL'S. By R. DOWLING.

VIVA. By MRS FORRESTER.

WHAT HAST THOU DONE? By J. FITZGERALD MOLLOY.

Novels. Price 1s. In Pictorial Wrappers.

A CHARGE FROM THE GRAVE. By SOMERVILLE GIBNEY.

AT THE ELEVENTH HOUR. By E. T. PICKERING.

BAG OF DIAMONDS. By G. M. FENN.

BLIND JUSTICE. By HELEN MATHERS.

DEVLIN THE BARBER. By B. L. FARJEON.

DR BERNARD ST. VINCENT: A Sensational Story of Sydney. By HUME NISBET.

EVE AT THE WHEEL. By G. M. FENN.

FATAL HOUSE, THE. By ALICE CORKRAN.

FOG PRINCES, THE. By FLORENCE WARDEN.

GREAT HESPER, THE. By FRANK BARRETT.

HIS OTHER SELF. By E. J. GOODMAN, Author of 'Too Curious.'

HOUSE OF TEARS, A. By EDMUND DOWNEY.

LADY VALWORTH'S DIAMONDS. By the Author of 'Molly Bawn."

LITTLE TU'PENNY. By the Author of 'Mehalah.'

MISS TODD'S DREAM. By MRS HUDDLESTON.

OLIVER'S BRIDE. By MRS OLIPHANT.

PRINCE OF DARKNESS, A. By FLORENCE WARDEN.

PROPOSALS; being a Maiden Meditation.

SCHOOL BOARD ESSAYS. By EMANUEL KINK.

SKELETON KEY, THE. By RICHARD DOWLING.

SUSPICION: A Strange Story. By CHRISTIAN LYS.

SWOOP OF THE EAGLES: An Episode in the Secret History of Europe.

VOYAGE OF THE ARK, THE. By F. M. ALLEN.

WHAT WAS IT? By FITZJAMES O'BRIEN.

WARD & DOWNEY, 12 York Street, Covent Garden, London

WARD & DOWNEY'S
CATALOGUE.

THE NEW SIXPENNY MAGAZINE
"EAST & WEST."

Among the contributors to EAST & WEST *are :—*

GRANT ALLEN.
F M. ALLEN.
ANNIE ARMITT.
S. BARING-GOULD.
MATHILDE BLIND.
PROFESSOR CHURCH.
C. F GORDON-CUMMING.
RICHARD DOWLING.
G. MANVILLE FENN.
R. E. FRANCILLON.
SOMERVILLE GIBNEY.
BRET HARTE.
KATHARINE S. MACQUOID.
THOMAS R. MACQUOID.

JEANNE MAIRET.
HELEN MATHERS.
L. T. MEADE.
MRS. MOLESWORTH.
ROSA MULHOLLAND.
W. E. NORRIS.
MRS. PARR.
MRS. PIATT
WILLIAM SHARP.
THOMAS STANLEY.
W W STORY.
SARAH TYTLER.
KATHERINE TYNAN.
L. B. WALFORD.

*** MESSRS. WARD & DOWNEY'S *Illustrated Catalogue contains Portraits of the Author of "Mehalah," the Author of "Molly Bawn," G. W Appleton, Frank Barrett, Robert Buchanan, Mrs. Lovett Cameron, Mabel Collins, Mrs. B. M. Croker, J. D. Delille, Richard Dowling, Charles Du Val, B. L. Farjeon, George Manville Fenn, Somerville Gibney, James Grant, Victor Hugo, Bret Harte, Richard Ashe King ("Basil"), Mrs. Macquoid, Fitzgerald Molloy, Christie Murray, O'Neill Daunt, John Augustus O'Shea, Mrs. Panton, James Payn, F. C. Philips, Mrs. Riddell, Blanche Roosevelt, George Sand, Florence Warden, William Westall, and Harry Furniss.*

NEW ILLUSTRATED BOOKS IN

PREPARATION.

PICTURESQUE LONDON. By PERCY FITZGERALD.
With about 100 Illustrations.

SOCIAL ENGLAND UNDER THE REGENCY
By JOHN ASHTON. Profusely Illustrated.

AT RANDOM : Sketches of Travel. By G. MACQUOID.
Illustrated by THOS. R. MACQUOID.

A MEMOIR OF CAPTAIN MAYNE REID. By his
WIDOW.

MEMORIES OF THE MONTH. By HUME NISBET.
With Photogravure Frontispiece, twelve whole page, and numerous
smaller Illustrations.

THE FLOATING PRINCE, and other Fairy Tales.
By the Author of " Rudder Grange." With Forty Illustrations.

TING-A-LING TALES. By FRANK R. STOCKTON.

AN ARTIST'S TOUR IN NORTH AND CENTRAL
AMERICA AND IN THE SANDWICH ISLANDS. By
B. KROUPA. Profusely Illustrated by the Author.

WARD & DOWNEY'S NEW BOOKS.

Price 36s.

THE LIFE AND LETTERS OF GEORGE SAND.
3 vols. Demy 8vo. With six Portraits.

Price 31s. 6d.

An *Édition de Luxe* of Mr. F. C. Philips's Novel,

AS IN A LOOKING GLASS. With original Illustrations by G. du Maurier. Extra crown quarto.

Three-Volume Novels. Price 31s. 6d.

AN ISLE OF SURREY. By Richard Dowling.
AT THE MOMENT OF VICTORY By C. L. Pirkis.
A YOUNG GIRL'S LIFE. By B. L. Farjeon.
BIRCHDENE. By William Westall.
BROUGHTON. By A. S. Arnold.
COMMON CLAY. By Mrs. Herbert Martin.
COPPER QUEEN, THE. By Blanche Roosevelt.
GOLD OF OPHIR, THE. By Elizabeth J. Lysaght.
GRAYSTONES. By Mrs. Riddell. [In the press.
HER TWO MILLIONS. By William Westall.
IN BLACK AND WHITE. By Percy Hulburd.
IN DURANCE VILE. By the Author of "Molly Bawn."

Three-Volume Novels (*continued*).

IN SIGHT OF LAND. By LADY DUFFUS HARDY.

LADY STELLA AND HER LOVER. By HENRY SOLLY.

LASS THAT LOVED A SOLDIER, THE. By G. M. FENN.

LUCINDA. By MAJOR WHITE.

MAN WITH A SHADOW, THE. By G. M. FENN.

'MID SURREY HILLS. By A. C. BICKLEY.

MIND, BODY, AND ESTATE. By MRS. NOTLEY.

MIRACLE GOLD. By RICHARD DOWLING.

MOLLY'S STORY By FRANK MERRYFIELD.

MONICA. By E. EVERETT-GREEN.

OF HIGH DESCENT By G. MANVILLE FENN.

ONE FOR THE OTHER. By ESME STUART.

PIT TOWN CORONET, THE. By CHAS. J. WILLS.

POWER OF THE HAND, THE. By MRS. NOTLEY.

ROY'S REPENTANCE. By ADELINE SARGEANT.

SEX TO THE LAST By PERCY FENDALL.

SHADOWED LIFE, A. By R. ASHE KING ("BASIL").

SIR JAMES APPLEBY By MRS. MACQUOID.

SPIDERS AND FLIES. By PERCY FENDALL.

STORY OF A MARRIAGE. By L. BALDWIN.

STRANGE AFFAIR, A. By W OUTRAM TRISTRAM.

THE TWO PARDONS. By HENRY SCOTT VINCE.

TRUST BETRAYED, A. By JOHN TIPTON.

UNCLE BOB'S NIECE. By LESLIE KEITH.

VOICE IN THE WILDERNESS, A. By CAROLINE FOTHERGILL.

Price 30s.

DUC DE BROGLIE: The Personal Recollections of.
2 vols., demy 8vo. With a Steel Portrait.

EDMUND KEAN: Life and Adventures of. By J. FITZ-
GERALD MOLLOY. 2 vols., demy 8vo. Limited Edition, printed
on antique laid paper, and handsomely bound in cloth gilt.

THE EMPRESS MARIA THERESA. From the
French of the Duc de Broglie. By Mrs. CASHEL HOEY. 2 vols.
[*In the press.*

UNPOPULAR KING, THE: The Life and Times of
Richard III. By ALFRED O. LEGGE. 2 vols., demy 8vo. With
sixteen Illustrations.

Price 25s.

LOVES AND MARRIAGES OF GREAT MEN. By
T. F. THISTLETON DYER. 2 vols.

HEALING ART, THE: Chapters on Medicine and
Medical Celebrities, from the Earliest Times to the Present Day.
By W. H. DAVENPORT ADAMS. Second edition. 2 vols., demy 8vo.

ROYALTY RESTORED; or, London under Charles II.
By J. FITZGERALD MOLLOY. 2 vols., large crown 8vo. With twelve
Portraits.

Price 21s.

AN ARTIST'S TOUR IN NORTH AND CENTRAL
AMERICA AND IN THE SANDWICH ISLANDS. By B.
KROUPA. Profusely Illustrated by the Author. [*Just ready.*

CLERICAL AND LITERARY RECOLLECTIONS.
By the Author of "Three-Cornered Essays." 2 vols.

COSMOPOLITAN RECOLLECTIONS. By the
Author of "Random Recollections by a Cosmopolitan." 2 vols.

EDMUND KEAN: Life and Adventures of. By J FITZ-
GERALD MOLLOY. 2 vols.

IRONBOUND CITY, AN: Five Months of Peril and
Privation in Besieged Paris. By JOHN AUGUSTUS O'SHEA. 2 vols.

JOHN WILKES: Life and Times of. By PERCY FITZ-
GERALD. 2 vols. With Four Portraits.

Price 21s. (*continued*)

LEAVES FROM THE LIFE OF A SPECIAL
CORRESPONDENT. By JOHN AUGUSTUS O'SHEA. 2 vols.

MEMORIES OF THE MONTH. By HUME NISBET.
With Photogravure Frontispiece, Twelve whole page, and numerous
smaller Illustrations by the Author. Edition limited to 250 copies.

ROMANTIC SPAIN: A Record of Personal Experiences.
By JOHN AUGUSTUS O'SHEA. 2 vols.

SHELLEY: The Man and the Poet. Translated from
the French of FELIX RABBE. 2 vols.

A YEAR IN THE GREAT REPUBLIC. By E.
KATHARINE BATES. 2 vols.

Two-Volume Novels. Price 21s.

COSETTE. By MRS. MACQUOID. [*In January.*

FIRE. By MRS. DIEHL, Author of "The Garden of
Eden."

FOR FREEDOM. By TIGHE HOPKINS.

FOR ONE AND THE WORLD. By M. BETHAM-
EDWARDS.

HEATHCOTE. By ELLA MACMAHON.

LEAL LASS, A. By R. ASHE KING ("BASIL").

LOOSE REIN, A: A Story of the Stable and the Stage.
By FRANK HUDSON.

MAD WORLD, A. By FRANK HUDSON.

TANGLED CHAIN, A. By MRS. PANTON.

TWIN SOUL, THE. By DR. CHARLES MACKAY.

Price 12s.

ALIENS, THE. By HENRY F KEENAN. 2 vols.

BROWNIE'S PLOT By THOMAS COBB.

JOHN FORD: His Faults and His Follies. By FRANK
BARRETT. 2 vols.

KALEIDOSCOPE: Shifting Scenes from East to West.
By E. KATHARINE BATES. Demy 8vo.

ROGER FERRON. By MRS. MACQUOID. 2 vols.

Price 10s. 6d.

CREATION OR EVOLUTION? A Philosophical Enquiry. By GEORGE TICKNOR CURTIS. Demy 8vo.

RANDOM RECOLLECTIONS OF COURTS AND SOCIETY. By a Cosmopolitan. Demy 8vo.

'TWIXT OLD TIMES AND NEW By the BARON DE MALORTIE.

Price 9s.

ROBERTSON OF BRIGHTON : with some Notices of his Times and his Contemporaries. By the REV. F ARNOLD B.A. Post 8vo.

Price 7s. 6d.

DUELLING DAYS IN THE ARMY By WILLIAM DOUGLAS. Imperial 16mo.

GREEK FOLK SONGS. With an Essay on the Science of Folk Lore. By J. S. STUART GLENNIE. New Edition. Demy 8vo.

IN RUSSIAN AND FRENCH PRISONS. By PRINCE KROPOTKIN. Large post 8vo.

MODERATE MAN, THE ; and other Humorous Poems. By EDWIN HAMILTON. With original Illustrations by HARRY FURNISS. Handsomely bound. Foolscap quarto.

OLD AND NEW SPAIN. By DR. HENRY M. FIELD. With Map. Demy 8vo.

OLD COURT LIFE IN FRANCE ; or, France under the Bourbons. By MRS. FRANCES ELLIOTT. With twenty whole-page Engravings. Royal 8vo.

SONGS FROM THE NOVELISTS. Collected and Edited and with Notes by W. DAVENPORT ADAMS. Printed in brown ink on hand-made paper and handsomely bound. Foolscap quarto.

VERDI, MILAN, AND OTHELLO : a short Life of Verdi. By BLANCHE ROOSEVELT. With eighteen Illustrations. Imperial 16mo, gilt top.

Price 6s.

ANCIENT LEGENDS OF IRELAND. By LADY WILDE.

AUSTRALIAN IN LONDON, THE. By J. F. HOGAN.

BYE-PATHS AND CROSS ROADS. By MRS. PANTON.

CATHEDRAL DAYS: A Tour through Southern England. By ANNA BOWMAN DODD. With numerous Illustrations.

CHARMS, OMENS, AND SUPERSTITIONS OF IRELAND. By LADY WILDE.

CHILDREN'S STORIES IN ENGLISH LITERATURE. By HENRIETTA C. WRIGHT.

COURT LIFE BELOW STAIRS; or, London under the First Georges. By J. FITZGERALD MOLLOY.

COURT LIFE BELOW STAIRS; or, London under the Last Georges. By J. FITZGERALD MOLLOY.

DUST AND DIAMONDS. By THOMAS PURNELL.

EIGHTY FIVE YEARS OF IRISH HISTORY. By W J. O'NEILL DAUNT.

EMPEROR WILLIAM, THE: The Story of a Great King and a good Man. By the late DR. G. L. M. STRAUSS.

EYES OF THE THAMES, THE: Picturesque Studies of Out-of-the-way Places. By ARTHUR T. PASK.

FAMOUS ENGLISH PLAYS: With some Account of their Origin and their Authors. By J. FITZGERALD MOLLOY.

FLOATING PRINCE, THE. By FRANK R. STOCKTON. With Forty Illustrations.

FRANÇOIS LISZT : Recollections of a Compatriot. By MADAM JANKA WOHL.

FROM KITCHEN TO GARRET: Hints to Young Householders. By MRS. PANTON.

INDOLENT ESSAYS. By RICHARD DOWLING.

IRISH INDUSTRIES, GLIMPSES OF By DR. J. BOWLES DALY.

LITTLE PEOPLE : Their Homes in Meadows, Woods, and Waters. By STELLA HOOK. Illustrated by D. and H. BEARD.

Price 6s.

LIVING PARIS: A Guide to the Manners, Monuments, and Institutions of the People. By "ALB." With Maps and Plans.

LOOK ROUND LITERATURE, A. By ROBERT BUCHANAN.

MARRIAGE AND HEREDITY; or, Some Aspects of Social Evolution. By J. F NISBET.

MAYNE REID, THE LATE CAPTAIN. A Memoir. By his WIDOW.

MEMOIRS OF AN ARABIAN PRINCESS, THE. An Autobiography. By the PRINCESS EMILY OF ZANZIBAR.

NOOKS AND CORNERS. A companion book to "From Kitchen to Garret." By MRS. PANTON.

OPERATIC TALES. By MAJOR-GENERAL CHESNEY.

RECOLLECTIONS OF A COUNTRY JOURNALIST. By THOMAS FROST. New Edition.

RED HUGH'S CAPTIVITY A Picture of Ireland, Social and Political, in the reign of Queen Elizabeth. By STANDISH O'GRADY.

ROYALTY RESTORED; or, London under Charles the Second. By J. FITZGERALD MOLLOY.

RUSSIA UNDER THE TZARS. By STEPNIAK.

SIX MONTHS IN THE HEJAZ: An Account of the Pilgrimages to Meccah and Medinah performed by the Author. By JOHN F KEANE.

STORIES OF THE GREAT SCIENTISTS. By HENRIETTA C. WRIGHT. With Eight Portraits.

STORY OF CARLYLE'S LIFE, THE. By A. S. ARNOLD.

THREE YEARS OF A WANDERER'S LIFE. By JOHN F KEANE.

TRAVELS IN THE INTERIOR. An attempt to teach the Anatomy and Physiology of the Human Body in a Novel and Entertaining Manner. Edited by a London Physician. Illustrated by HARRY FURNISS.

VICTOR HUGO: His Life and Work. By GEORGE BARNETT SMITH. With an Engraved Portrait of Hugo.

One-Volume Novels. Price 6s.

ALIENS, THE. By Henry F. Keenan.

AT THE RED GLOVE. By Mrs. Macquoid. Illustrated by C. S. Reinhart.

AUDREY FERRIS. By Frances A. Gerard.

BEACHCOMBERS, THE; or, Slave-Trading under the Union Jack. By Gilbert Bishop. Illustrated by Hume Nisbet.

CHILCOTES, THE. By Leslie Keith.

DESPERATE REMEDIES. By Thomas Hardy.

EIGHT BELLS. By Hume Nisbet. Illustrated by the Author.

IDLE TALES. By Mrs. Riddell.

JOHN O' LONDON By Somerville Gibney. Illustrated by M. Fitzgerald.

LAND OF THE HIBISCUS BLOSSOM, THE. By Hume Nisbet. Illustrated by the Author.

LEONORA. By William V Herbert.

LIL LORIMER. By Theo. Gift.

LUCK AT THE DIAMOND FIELDS. By D. J Belgrave.

MASTER OF RYLANDS, THE. By Lucy Leeds.

MIKE FLETCHER. By George Moore.

MRS. RUMBOLD'S SECRET By Mrs. Macquoid.

PRINCESS SUNSHINE. By Mrs. Riddell.

QUESTION OF CAIN, THE. By Mrs. Cashel Hoey.

ROBERT HOLT'S ILLUSION By Mary Linskill.

RUINED RACE, A. By Mrs. Sigerson.

SFORZA. By the Author of "Valentino."

STRANGEST JOURNEY OF MY LIFE, THE. By F Pigot.

STORY OF ANTONY GRACE, THE. By George Manville Fenn. Illustrated by Gordon Browne.

WHEAL CERTAINTY: A Cornish story. By John Cahill.

WYVERN MYSTERY, THE. By J. S. Le Fanu. Illustrated by B. S. Le Fanu.

Price 5s.

A TALE OF THREE NATIONS. By J. F Hodgetts.

ANGÈLE'S TEMPTERS: A Novel. By Isaac Teller.

THE CURSE OF KOSHIU: A Story of Japan. By the Hon. Lewis Wingfield.

GLORINDA: A Story. By Anna Bowman Dodd.

JOHN BROWN AND LARRY LOHENGRIN: A Tale with Two Heroes. By William Westall.

IGNORANT ESSAYS. By Richard Dowling.

NIGEL FORTESCUE; or, The Hunted Man. By William Westall.

ORANGES AND ALLIGATORS: Life in South Florida. By Iza Duffus Hardy.

ORIGIN OF PLUM PUDDING, THE. By Frank Hudson. With Coloured Illustrations by Gordon Browne.

A PRINCE OF THE BLOOD. By James Payn.

Price 3s. 6d.

ARM-CHAIR ESSAYS. By F. Arnold.

BRAVE MEN IN ACTION: Thrilling Stories of the British Flag. By Stephen J. Mackenna and John Augustus O'Shea.

CANDIDATE'S LATIN GRAMMAR, THE. By J. Percy Reed, M.A.

CHAMELEON, THE: Fugitive Fancies on many Coloured Matters. By Charles J. Dunphie.

FIFTY YEARS OF A GOOD QUEEN'S REIGN. By A. H. Wall. With six Portraits. Gilt edges, 4s. 6d.

GOLDEN SOUTH, THE. Memories of Home Life in Australia. By " Lyth."

ORIGINAL, THE. By Thomas Walker. With an Introduction by Richard Dowling.

OURSELVES AND OUR NEIGHBOURS: Short Chats on Social Topics. By Louise Chandler Moulton.

PARIS BY DAY AND NIGHT. By Anglo-Parisian.

PAST, PRESENT, AND FUTURE: An Historical Inquiry. By F. L. C. King.

RANDOM RECOLLECTIONS OF COURTS AND SOCIETY. By a Cosmopolitan.

THREE-CORNERED ESSAYS. By F. Arnold.

One-Volume Novels. Price 3s. 6d.

ANCHOR WATCH YARNS. By F. M. ALLEN.
Illustrated by M. FITZGERALD.

BRANDON CARR; or, Life in the Transvaal. By MRS.
CAREY HOBSON. [*In the press.*

CATCHING A TARTAR. By G. W APPLETON.

DIANA BARRINGTON. By B. M. CROKER.

FOX AND THE GOOSE, THE: A Story of the
Curragh of Kildare. By J. P GLYNN.

FROZEN HEARTS. By G. W APPLETON.

IN JEOPARDY. By GEORGE MANVILLE FENN.

IN LUCK'S WAY. By BYRON WEBBER.

IN ONE TOWN. By E. DOWNEY.

JACK ALLYN'S FRIENDS. By G. W APPLETON.

LAST HURDLE, THE: A Story of Sporting and
Courting. By FRANK HUDSON.

LESS THAN KIN By J. E. PANTON.

LIEUTENANT BARNABAS. By FRANK BARRETT.

LOGIE TOWN. By SARAH TYTLER.

MISS ELVESTER'S GIRLS. By M. W PAXTON.

MY SPANISH SAILOR. By MARSHALL SAUNDERS.

MYSTERY OF KILLARD, THE. By RICHARD
DOWLING.

NEW RIVER, THE. By SOMERVILLE GIBNEY.

PASSAGES IN THE LIFE OF A LADY. By
HAMILTON AÏDÉ.

One-Volume Novels. Price 3s. 6d. *(continued)*.

RECOILING VENGEANCE, A. By FRANK BARRETT.
With Illustrations by E. J. BREWTNALL.

RED RUIN: A Tale of West African River Life. By
A. N. HOMER.

SPANISH GALLEON, THE. By F. C. BADRICK,
Author of "Starwood Hall."

TARTAN AND GOLD. By BYRON WEBBER.

THROUGH GREEN GLASSES. By F. M. ALLEN.
Illustrated Edition.

TING-A-LING TALES. By FRANK R. STOCKTON.

TWO PINCHES OF SNUFF By WILLIAM WESTALL.

WHERE TEMPESTS BLOW By M. W PAXTON.

WRECK OF THE ARGO; or, the Island Home.

Price 2s. 6d.

CRIME OF KESIAH KEENE, THE: A Novel. By
MRS. VERE CAMPBELL.

COMMON SENSE IN THE NURSERY By MARION
HARLAND.

DISHES AND DRINKS; or, Philosophy in the Kitchen.
By the late DR. G. L. M. STRAUSS.

FROM THE GREEN BAG. By F M. ALLEN.

IRISH IN AUSTRALIA, THE. By J. F. HOGAN.

LIVING PARIS. "Exhibition" Edition.

STORY OF MARY HERRIES, THE: A Novel.

THE OUTLAW OF ICELAND. By VICTOR HUGO.

Novels. Price 2s. In Picture Boards.

AN AUSTRALIAN HEROINE. By Mrs. Campbell Praed.

ANTONY GRACE. By G. Manville Fenn.

AS IN A LOOKING GLASS. By F. C. Philips.

BIRD OF PASSAGE, A. By B. M. Croker.

CANON LUCIFER. By J. D. Delille.

CHEQUERS, THE. By James Runciman.

COQUETTE'S CONQUEST, A. By " Basil."

DEAN AND HIS DAUGHTER, THE. By F C. Philips.

DINGY HOUSE AT KENSINGTON, THE.

DOUBLE CUNNING. By G. Manville Fenn.

DUKE'S SWEETHEART, THE. By R. Dowling.

EARLY FROST, AN By C. R. James.

FLOWER OF DOOM, THE. By M. Betham-Edwards.

FOLLY MORRISON. By Frank Barrett.

GREAT PORTER SQUARE. By B. L. Farjeon.

GRETCHEN By " Rita."

GRIF. By B. L. Farjeon.

HANDSOME JACK. By James Greenwood.

HER TWO MILLIONS. By William Westall.

HONEST DAVIE. By Frank Barrett.

HOUSE OF WHITE SHADOWS, THE. By B. L. Farjeon.

HUSBAND AND WIFE. By Marie Connor.

IN ONE TOWN By Edmund Downey.

IN A SILVER SEA. By B. L. Farjeon.

IN THE FLOWER OF HER YOUTH. By Mabel Collins.

JACK AND THREE JILLS. By F C. Philips.

LADYE NANCYE, THE. By " Rita."

LIFE'S MISTAKE, A. By Mrs. H. Lovett Cameron.

LOUISA. By K. S. Macquoid.

LUCKY YOUNG WOMAN, A. By F. C. Philips.

MAIDEN ALL FORLORN, A. By the Author of
" Molly Bawn."

MARVEL. By the Author of " Molly Bawn."

MASTER OF THE CEREMONIES, THE. By G. M.
FENN.

MENTAL STRUGGLE, A. By the Author of " Molly
Bawn."

MISER FAREBROTHER. By B. L. FARJEON.

MODERN CIRCE, A. By the Author of " Molly
Bawn."

MODERN MAGICIAN, A. By FITZGERALD MOLLOY.

NUN'S CURSE, THE. By MRS. RIDDELL.

OLD FACTORY, THE. By WILLIAM WESTALL.

ONE MAID'S MISCHIEF By G. M. FENN.

PRETTIEST WOMAN IN WARSAW, THE. By
MABEL COLLINS.

PRETTY MISS NEVILLE. By B. M. CROKER.

PROPER PRIDE. By B. M. CROKER.

RALPH NORBRECK'S TRUST By WILLIAM
WESTALL.

RED RYVINGTON. By WILLIAM WESTALL.

REIGNING FAVOURITE, A. By ANNIE THOMAS.

SACRED NUGGET, THE. By B. L. FARJEON.

SCHEHERAZADE. By the Author of " The House on
the Marsh."

SOCIAL VICISSITUDES. By F. C. PHILIPS.

TEMPEST DRIVEN. By RICHARD DOWLING.

TERRIBLE LEGACY, A. By G. W APPLETON.

THAT VILLAIN ROMEO. By J. FITZGERALD MOLLOY.

THIS MAN'S WIFE. By G. M. FENN.

THROUGH GREEN GLASSES. By F M. ALLEN.

TRAGEDY OF FEATHERSTONE, THE. By B. L.
FARJEON.

UNDER ST PAUL'S. By R. DOWLING.

VIVA. BY MRS. FORRESTER.

WHAT HAST THOU DONE ? By J. FITZGERALD
MOLLOY.

Novels. Price 1s.

A CHARGE FROM THE GRAVE. By SOMERVILLE GIBNEY.

AT THE ELEVENTH HOUR. By E. T PICKERING.

BAG OF DIAMONDS. By G. M. FENN.

BLIND JUSTICE. By HELEN MATHERS.

DEVLIN THE BARBER. By B. L. FARJEON.

DR. BERNARD ST VINCENT: A Sensational Story of Sydney. By HUME NISBET.

EVE AT THE WHEEL. By G. M. FENN.

FATAL HOUSE. THE. By ALICE CORKRAN.

FOG PRINCES, THE. By FLORENCE WARDEN.

GREAT HESPER, THE. By FRANK BARRETT.

HIS OTHER SELF By E. J. GOODMAN, Author of "Too Curious."

HOUSE OF TEARS, A. By EDMUND DOWNEY.

LADY VALWORTH'S DIAMONDS. By the Author of "Molly Bawn."

LITTLE TUPENNY By the Author of "Mehalah."

MISS TODD'S DREAM. By MRS. HUDDLESTON.

OLIVER'S BRIDE. By MRS. OLIPHANT.

PRINCE OF DARKNESS, A. By FLORENCE WARDEN.

PROPOSALS ; being a Maiden Meditation.

SCHOOL BOARD ESSAYS. By EMANUEL KINK.

SKELETON KEY, THE. By RICHARD DOWLING.

SUSPICION : A strange story. By CHRISTIAN LYS.

SWOOP OF THE EAGLES: An Episode in the Secret History of Europe.

VOYAGE OF THE ARK, THE. By F M. ALLEN.

WHAT WAS IT ? By FITZJAMES O'BRIEN.

WARD & DOWNEY, 12, York Street, Covent Garden, London.

Novello, Ewer & Co., Printers, London.

Ward & Downey's Illustrated Books.

THE WYVERN MYSTERY. By J. Sheridan Le Fanu. Illustrated by B. S. Le Fanu. 6s.

AS IN A LOOKING GLASS. By F. C. Philips. Illustrated by G. du Maurier. 31s. 6d.

EIGHT BELLS: a Story of the Sea. By Hume Nisbet. Illustrated by the Author. 6s.

THE LAND OF THE HIBISCUS BLOSSOM: a Yarn of New Guinea. By Hume Nisbet. Illustrated by the Author. 6s.

THE ORIGIN OF PLUM PUDDING. By Frank Hudson. Illustrated by Gordon Browne. 5s.

LITTLE PEOPLE AND THEIR HOMES IN MEADOWS, WOODS, AND WATER. By Stella J. Hook. Illustrated by D. and H. Beard. 6s.

AT THE RED GLOVE. By Katharine S. Macquoid. Illustrated by C. S. Reinhart. Cloth gilt. 6s.

THE MODERATE MAN, AND OTHER HUMOROUS VERSES. By Edwin Hamilton. Illustrated by Harry Furniss. 7s. 6d.

TRAVELS IN THE INTERIOR. Edited by a London Physician. Illustrated by Harry Furniss. 6s.

JOHN O' LONDON: a Story of the Days of Roger Bacon. Illustrated by M. Fitzgerald. 6s.

THROUGH GREEN GLASSES. By F. M. Allen. Illustrated by M. Fitzgerald. 3s. 6d.

ANCHOR WATCH YARNS. By F. M. Allen. Illustrated by M. Fitzgerald. 3s. 6d.

VERDI, MILAN, AND "OTHELLO": a Short Life of Verdi. By Blanche Roosevelt. Profusely Illustrated. 7s. 6d.

CATHEDRAL DAYS: a Tour in Southern England. By Anna Bowman Dodd. With Illustrations from Sketches and Photographs. 6s.

OLD COURT LIFE IN FRANCE. By Mrs. Frances Elliott. Illustrated by A. Fredericks. 7s. 6d.

12, YORK STREET, COVENT GARDEN, LONDON, W.C.

TWO SHILLING NOVELS.

HER TWO MILLIONS. By W. Westall.
A MODERN CIRCE. By the Author of "Molly Bawn."
THE STORY OF ANTONY GRACE. By G. Manville Fenn.
A MODERN MAGICIAN. By J. Molloy.
GRETCHEN. By Rita.
SCHEHERAZADE. By Florence Warden.
THIS MAN'S WIFE. By G. Manville Fenn.
THROUGH GREEN GLASSES. By F. M. Allen.
THE SACRED NUGGET. By B. L. Farjeon.
A REIGNING FAVOURITE. By Annie Thomas.
A LIFE'S MISTAKE. By Mrs. H. Lovett Cameron.
ONE MAID'S MISCHIEF. By G. Manville Fenn.
A MENTAL STRUGGLE. By the Author of "Molly Bawn."
HANDSOME JACK. By James Greenwood.
TEMPEST DRIVEN. By Richard Dowling.
A TERRIBLE LEGACY. By G. W. Appleton.
DOUBLE CUNNING. By G. Manville Fenn.
THE DINGY HOUSE AT KENSINGTON.
THE OLD FACTORY. By William Westall.
RED RYVINGTON. By William Westall.
RALPH NORBECK'S TRUST. By William Westall.
THE CHEQUERS. By James Runciman.
CANON LUCIFER. By J. D. Delille.
THAT VILLAIN ROMEO. By Fitzgerald Molloy.
WHAT HAST THOU DONE? By Fitzgerald Molloy.
LOUISA. By K. S. Macquoid.
THE LADYE NANCYE. By "Rita."
A LUCKY YOUNG WOMAN. By F. C. Philips.
THE DEAN AND HIS DAUGHTER. By F. C. Philips.
JACK AND THREE JILLS. By F. C. Philips.
AS IN A LOOKING GLASS. By F. C. Philips.
SOCIAL VICISSITUDES. By F. C. Philips.
PROPER PRIDE. By B. M. Croker.
PRETTY MISS NEVILLE. By B. M. Croker.
MISS GASCOIGNE. By Mrs. Riddell.
A MAIDEN ALL FORLORN. By the Author of "Molly Bawn."
HER WEEK'S AMUSEMENT. By the Author of "Molly Bawn."
A COQUETTE'S CONQUEST. By "Basil."
IN A SILVER SEA. By B. L. Farjeon.
GREAT PORTER SQUARE. By B. L. Farjeon.
THE HOUSE OF WHITE SHADOWS. By B. L. Farjeon.
GRIF. By B. L. Farjeon.
SNOWBOUND AT EAGLE'S. By Bret Harte.
VIVA. By Mrs. Forrester.
FOLLY MORRISON. By Frank Barrett.
HONEST DAVIE. By Frank Barrett.
UNDER ST. PAUL'S. By R. Dowling.

WARD & DOWNEY'S SHILLING BOOKS.

AT THE ELEVENTH HOUR. By E. T. Pickering.

THE SWOOP OF THE EAGLES: An Episode from the Secret History of Europe.

THE FOG PRINCES. By Florence Warden.

SUSPICION. By Christian Lys.

DR. BERNARD ST. VINCENT. By Hume Nisbet.

WHAT WAS IT? By Fitzjames O'Brien.

THE FATAL HOUSE. By Alice Corkran.

THE MYSTERY OF CROOMBER. By A. Conan Doyle.

DEVLIN THE BARBER. By B. L. Farjeon.

THE VOYAGE OF THE ARK. By F M. Allen.

SCHOOL BOARD ESSAYS. By Emanuel Kink, Author of "Babies and Ladders."

PROPOSALS: Being a Maiden Meditation.

AN IMPECUNIOUS LADY. By Mrs. Forrester.

THE GREAT HESPER. By Frank Barrett.

A BAG OF DIAMONDS. By G. M. Fenn.

THE DARK HOUSE. By G. M. Fenn. Third Edition.

EVE AT THE WHEEL. By G. M. Fenn.

THE CHAPLAIN'S CRAZE. By G. M. Fenn.

LITTLE TU'PENNY. By the Author of "Mehalah."

A HOUSE OF TEARS. By E. Downey. 12th Edition.

LADY VALWORTH'S DIAMONDS. By the Author of "Phyllis." Third Edition.

A PRINCE OF DARKNESS. By the Author of "The House on the Marsh." Fifth Edition.

THE SKELETON KEY. By R. Dowling.

MOLKA. By B. L. Farjeon.

OLIVER'S BRIDE. By Mrs. Oliphant.

WITH A SHOW THROUGH SOUTHERN AFRICA. By Charles Du Val.

WIT AND WISDOM OF THE LATE EMPEROR WILLIAM. Cloth.

DANCERS AND DANCING; or, Grace and Folly. By Edward Scott.

12, YORK STREET, COVENT GARDEN, LONDON, W.C.

www.ingramcontent.com/pod-product-compliance
Lightning Source LLC
Chambersburg PA
CBHW060552030726
47498CB00005B/1362